The bullies always managed to pick on him, but this time, he was fighting back...

The cafeteria was a death trap and both hunters and prey knew it. All the students were required to be in the lunch room until the bell rang and the two worthless lunch room teacher's aids, instead of being on guard, would sit at their own table up front and yak for the entire forty minutes.

Gregory had tried to sit at the table next to them but their eyes burned him. They would relentlessly stare, intent on seeing into his mind. Gregory would not allow that. He was careful not to look them in the eyes, so he only stole glances with his peripheral vision, but finally, he decided he couldn't stay near them and, hence, was on his own at lunch. Generally, he would hide in a back corner where extra chairs were stacked up. He would quickly rearrange them into a small fort with one chair to sit on and another as his lunch table. From this vantage point, he could see the entire cafeteria and no one could sneak up on him. If someone tried an attack on his fortress, he had a secret weapon.

The Pack entered a few minutes after he did and sat down at their regular table. This was expected as they always ate before the hunt. With full bellies their strength would rise, and then they'd be ready. Gregory munched down his own ham and cheese sandwich as he watched them do the same. Every once in a while, they would take peeks in his direction. They were plotting, but Gregory wasn't stupid. This time, he'd see them coming and he had an ace up his sleeve. His plan might not take out all of them but it would neutralize at least one or two and give him a moment to escape. They got him earlier but not this time.

In a toxic world of peer pressure, torment, and rivalry, justice is just one click away for these three high-school underdogs. Thousands of miles apart from each other, each trapped in his own circle of hell, they find solace in a mysterious online ally named Nikki who strokes their fragile egos and urges them to realize their ultimate revenge fantasies. How far will the three outcasts go to impress the best friend they never met? Set in the grotesque and volatile e-universe, where nothing is what it seems, *The Online Boys* is a disturbing and psychologically authentic cyber-thriller for both bullies and victims.

KUDOS for *The Online Boys*

In *The Online Boys* by Daniel Shebses, Nikki is an abused high-school student, bullied by some of the other students. So Nikki retreats to online teen chat rooms and meets several boys who are also bullied. The boys take comfort from Nikki's compassion and understanding and they are the only friends that Nikki has. But when Nikki and the lost boys (sounds like a rock and roll band, doesn't it?) finally decide to take justice into their own hands, things don't quite turn out like they plan—or like Nikki promised. Shebses has written a heart-wrenching and poignant story of high school bullying and the adverse effects that it can have on everyone it touches, even those who don't participate in the bullying, but just stand by and let others do it. It's a story that everyone should read, be they bully, victim, or bystander. ~ *Taylor Jones, Reviewer*

The Online Boys by Daniel Shebses is a realistic look at high school bullying. While it is no secret that kids can be, and often are, cruel, I doubt that few adults really understand what it is liked to bullied in high school where so much of your self-esteem is dependent on how you are treated, and viewed, by your peers. There is no question that bullying is rampant in the world today, and that few people, children or adults, are really equipped to deal with it. Shebses give us a chilling look at what the tragic consequences can be if bullying goes unchecked. It is thought-provoking and heart-breaking tale. I was a tad disappointed in the ending, but then maybe I'm just more blood-thirsty than most. ~ *Regan Murphy, Reviewer*

ACKNOWLEDGEMENTS

Thank you to my parents for your endless support and to Marina Neary for your wonderful advice.

THE ONLINE BOYS

Daniel Shebses

A Black Opal Books Publication

THE ONLINE BOYS

CHAPTER 1

Gregory and Nikki

*L*ogging onto *Automatic Chatting Utility…*
Welcome to ACU

M@nikM@nn: *Nikki you there?*
TheGorgeousOne: *yup, How r u greg*
M@nikM@nn: *no good, bad day at school*
TheGorgeousOne: *What happened?*
TheGorgeousOne: *Were u picked on*
M@nikM@nn: *yea like every day. How do you stand it? Are girls as mean as boys?*

TheGorgeousOne*: I may be a girl, but boys and girls hate me*

M@nikM@nn: *Your the only girl that talks to me. I'm glad we found each other online*

TheGorgeousOne: *one day we'll get them all! We can't help being who we are*

M@nikM@nn: *Yeah, I'm kinda spazzy and all but Im a good guy. I'm sure you're a nice girl in real life too.*

TheGorgeousOne: *I could of been nice, now I hate them all!*

M@nikM@nn: *Yeah, I could of been to. now I hate them. Today they made fun of me for talking to myself at my locker. It helps me remember things. And if I don't do something right I have to do it again.*

TheGorgeousOne: *Its not your fault, I don't fit in, but now I don't try. I have friends online like you.*

M@nikM@nn: *yeah I'm glad I have you to talk to. My mom is always busy and stuff. I like talking online anyway. its hard to talk to people in the face. Im not good at it.*

TheGorgeousOne: *That's what makes me so angry for you. Nasty boys see a shy boy like you and pick on him for it. Nasty boys!*

M@nikM@nn: *They push me call me retard, throw my books on the floor sometimes they hit me in the head and say It will help me. I cant do anything.*

TheGorgeousOne: *Don't worry, we are both smarter*

than them. Eventually we'll get them.

M@nikM@nn: *When? I have a gun, My dad left it when he left I know where it is*

TheGorgeousOne: *PLeaeeazze, stay calm sweety, I know your hurting. Me too but it isn't the right time. Be patient and trust me. Do you trust me?*

M@nikM@nn: *yes I trust you. You're the only one I trust you're the only one who cares about me*

TheGorgeousOne: *I know your hurting sweety. I love you Everything is so unfair but for the moment I want you to relax and play your videogames. Your good at that and it makes you happy.*

M@nikM@nn: *It's the only thing im good at nothing else.*

TheGorgeousOne: *not true. You make me laugh and you make me happy by talking to me. Isn't that important?*

M@nikM@nn: *yeah it is, you make me happy too, can you come to Odessa ny to meet me?*

TheGorgeousOne*: Sorry Sweety Im stuck in bumblescum Ohio*

M@nikM@nn: *lol you mean Parkins Ohio*

TheGorgeousOne: *I like my name better*

M@nikM@nn: *me too*

TheGorgeousOne: *I have to get my beauty sleep now. R U feeling better?*

M@nikM@nn: *I guess goodnight*

TheGorgeousOne: *G'Night sweety play your video games to relax*

M@nikM@nn: *ok luv ya*

TheGorgeousOne is offline

CHAPTER 2

The Spazz

Gregory Manink stepped away from his bedroom computer, feeling a bit more content. Chatting with Nikki always put him in a better mood after a miserable day at school. Although he was tolerated by some, she was his only friend, having met in a teen chat room several months earlier. She was his only experience with girls, as most would just roll their eyes at him and giggle with contempt. One day when he worked up the courage, he would ask Nikki to be his girlfriend, if only online. *She might agree to it*, Gregory told himself. She was alone too. Maybe they could even play video games together online and pretend the nasty people who taunted them so mercilessly were the bad guys. Gregory smiled. How he would love to be able to embrace her hand in one of his, while having a gun in the other.

Video games would calm his nerves. They always did. But first, he had to use the bathroom. Before leaving his bedroom, with his right thumb and middle finger, he flicked each finger on his left hand, starting with the left thumb and ending at the pinky. Once this task was completed, he used his left thumb and middle finger and completed the same ritual to each digit on the right hand, thumb to pinky. After fulfilling the second round of finger flips, he tapped his bedroom doorknob the required four times before opening it, and only then stepped out into the hall.

In between his room and the bathroom was his mother's home office where she worked day in and day out. It was after 8 p.m. and still she toiled. She made good money, but it was rare that she exited except for bathroom breaks and mail deliveries requiring a signature. The aroma of pre-packaged food crept from the office, as her desk usually doubled as her kitchen table, and a small microwave her cook. Gregory ate alone most nights with only the television as company, well, the television, video games, and Nikki.

Gregory thought he caught the pungent odor of over-cooked broccoli as he stepped into the bathroom. So focused was he on the broccoli's stench, that only after he unzipped his pants did Gregory realize his error. Beads of sweat emerged across his forehead and he turned back to the doorway, horrified by his mistake. He hadn't been paying attention and now was on the verge of a full blown panic. Had he entered the bathroom left foot first or right foot first? He couldn't remember, and he cursed his stupidity. Things had to be done properly. Which foot had he stepped into the bathroom with first? It should have been the right foot, but it could have been the left, and now his breathing quickened.

This wouldn't do at all. All bathrooms had to be entered right foot first! That was the proper way of doing things and it must be done. He zipped up his pants and stepped out of the bathroom. Once back in the hall, he relaxed a bit, realizing he had not urinated yet and could still correct himself. With a deep breath, he stepped back into the bathroom, right foot first. He smiled. Everything was proper now and he went about his business.

On returning to his bedroom, he casually entered left foot first. It didn't matter which foot entered a bedroom first, or a kitchen, or classroom, or any other room. Only bathrooms had to be entered right foot first. He closed the bedroom door, careful to remember the mandatory four taps on the knob.

Before playing video games, he decided to change into his pajamas. First, he pulled off his T-shirt and, bit-ing his lip, threw it across the room toward the open hamper. Thankfully, it soared in. He had only one shot to get the shirt into the hamper, otherwise he'd have a sleepless night.

Next, he removed his pants and threw them toward the hamper, this time missing. Gregory sighed. It may not have been as dire to get the pants into the hamper in one shot as it was the shirt, but missing was annoying, none the less. He walked over to the side of the hamper where his pants had landed, picked them up, and walked back across the room. A second shot and another miss annoyed Gregory further. He walked back over, picked up his pants, and then returned to his shooting position. The third time was the charm and the pants now rested in the hamper. Finally, he pulled off his socks and boxers, gave the socks a good tug at each end, and walked them over to the hamper. Shirts and pants must always be thrown into the hamper, while socks and underwear could just be dropped in. That was the proper way of doing things.

Not wanting to be naked for very long, he opened his pajama drawer. Since tonight was Tuesday, that meant he would wear his red bed time shorts and T-shirt. After donning them, he looked farther into the drawer seeing his Wednesday black shorts and T-shirt as well as his Thursday blue shorts and T-shirt.

Friday would be red again, while Saturday, Sunday, and Monday he would wear his gray shorts and T-shirt.

Gregory smiled at the propriety of his pajama drawer.

Now in his pajamas, it was time to get busy with his video games. He loved them and he was good, very good. Nobody, save the anonymous gamers he went up against online, had any inkling of the kind of talent he possessed. Well, maybe the demons and aliens, and enemy soldiers he killed on a daily basis had a clue. They knew well. Sometimes he wondered how many murders he committed while playing his video games—hundreds, thousands, more? He could not be sure, but he definitely had spilled much virtual blood.

His library of games was extensive and he had all the various gaming systems needed to play any of them, from XBOX360 though GameCube and of course PlayStation 3. Video games made everything right naturally without any need for a proper way of doing things. He could just plug in the game and let the slaughter begin without worrying about his required rituals.

Now which one should he play? The Warriors, or NARC, or Killer 7, maybe Gears of War, 50 Cent: Bulletproof, Thrill Kill, Halo, Resident Evil, Halflife, Mad World? Perhaps, True Crime NYC, or Postal 2, or Hitman, Shadow Heart, Manhunt, or Solider of Fortune, God of War, Grand Theft Auto, Quake, or Crime Life: Gang War 3, Mortal Combat, or Doom, Driver, Duke Nukem 3D, Dead Rising, Wolfenstein, Blood, Requiem: Avenging Angel, The Punisher, or Silent Hill: Homecoming,

Phantasmagoria, Reservoir Dogs, Mafia II, Counter Strike, Shell Shock 2, Aliens Vs. Predator, Left 4 Dead 2, The Getaway.

Wide eyed, Gregory sported a rare smile, turned away, and grabbed a game at random. To hell with being proper! He gazed back to see that Doom was the lucky winner and he slipped it into his XBOX. Within seconds, he was killing dozens of demons a minute. No mercy, no remorse, simply beautiful blood and death for all who got in his way. Machine guns, rocket launchers, and gorgeous imaginary videogame weapons were his to control, his to slaughter with. These demons were no match for him. He was too good, too strong, too well armed. His body count rose by the second, followed by absolute ecstasy.

CHAPTER 3

Working Mom

Entombed within her office, Gregory's mother barely noticed the shuffling back and forth of her son out in the hall. Although it was late, the papers were still piled high on her desk and her email "in" box was stuffed. If she was lucky, maybe she'd get to bed by 1 a.m., at least that was what she hoped for. On more than one occasion it was a good deal later. As the bluish puff bags under her eyes and the bloodshot streaks within insinuated, a project manager at RC & J Associates never slept.

Since 8 a.m. she had been bound to her home office

desk, writing reports, entering numbers, answering emails, and making calls. The first of her two conference calls of the day had run far longer than expected, which cost her some time. It was some stupid accounting problem with the Rodriguez Concrete client. The idiot project manager handling that easy gem of an assignment had somehow screwed it up so and it fell on her to fix, which she did.

Gregory's mom sneered bitterly at the thought of that woman. Anyone else would have been fired after all the blunders and irresponsibility she had shown, but little miss princess was the daughter of the Vice President of RC & J Associates, and Daddy was just so proud of his little girl completing her rehab. And why shouldn't Daddy be proud? To be fair, some rehab patients were in and out for years and never got clean. Daddy's little girl, however, did it in a mere four tries. Oh well done, darling!

With the Rodriguez issue resolved, she was finally able to begin work on her major tasks of the day, which included setting up new accounts for three recently acquired clients: Sanborn Management, Avelis Co., and Indiana Electric. Ordinarily, three new accounts would never have fallen on one person, but unforeseen events had befallen the company. Originally, Gregory's mother was only slated to handle Sanborn Management, but then Sheila was diagnosed with breast cancer and Marge was in a serious car wreck. Although both women were doing well in treatment, all the company's clients for which they were responsible still had to be tended to and, with no money in the budget for temps, everyone in the New Accounts Department had to step up. Avelis Co. and Indiana Electric plopped into her lap right on top of her other large clients.

She had hours of work ahead of her but, at the very least, Gregory's mother could take satisfaction in knowing that she was making progress and nothing was being neglected. There had been some distractions, but the files for Sanborn Management and Avelis Co. were at last completed and emailed into Central Office. Indiana Electric was a bit more involved than the other two had been. It was a first for her as she had never handled a power company before and they possessed certain accounting procedures and technical terms that she was not familiar with. A few extra calls, emails, and internet searches had been needed. Although she still had a ways to go on Indiana Electric, she was making decent time and rewarded herself with a short stretching break, the first in several hours.

She rose from her desk and pushed her hands toward the ceiling, feeling the lovely cricks from her shoulders and spine as they stretched. She then bent over and touched her toes, taking a sense of pride that even at her age, she could still reach them. At times she ached after being hunched over her computer for too long. She really should improve her work station. Her desk was too high and her keyboard drawer too low. Still, if she wanted a new desk, she'd have to pay for it out of pocket. This was the standard desk the company provided for its home office employees. She did a few more twists and stretches, enjoying the bit of pain relaxing the muscles brought to her body.

The wage from her job was good, although she didn't enjoy the work. Sitting in front of a computer monitor with spreadsheets, emails, and numbers all day would be hell even for the most physically lazy of people. Before her husband left her for a woman almost twenty years her junior, he had really brought home the bacon. He worked as a high level executive at a large bank and made it possible for her to do the volunteer work that she loved, working in animal shelters. She had to admit to being spoiled, but in time late nights at his office turned into sleepovers at *her* house and soon he left. Her husband had always shown only minimal interest in Gregory, who she agreed could be a challenge, but he was still his son. He gave her the house in the divorce, but with his high powered lawyers, he regularly screwed her out of alimony. Determined to keep the house and her pride, she had accepted her present job and worked to the bone. Now she drudged late into the night like her husband once did and got to see Gregory about as often.

From beyond her door she thought she heard the faint sounds of Gregory's videogames. He kept the volume low and she was always grateful for the consideration. She didn't much like the videogames, but they kept him occupied on his many sleepless nights. He was always difficult like that, whether it was not sleeping, fidgeting, or some other compulsive behavior. There was no question that her Gregory was not like normal children. Meds and therapists did little to help.

After the divorce, her work had saved her from bitterness. It gave her an outlet and, although she worked like an abused sled dog, she was the top project manager in the company. Her ex-husband could suck on that for a while. She might not have been able to spend as much time with Gregory as she would have liked, but she was able to maintain a job and a home even without his money.

Proud of her achievements, she relaxed back into her chair and thought of Gregory again. She spent so much time in her office, when had she last really seen him? They had eaten breakfast together that morning, although he was usually on his own for dinner. He was a grown boy and could warm up his TV dinners himself. In that regard, he was very independent. Still, he didn't talk much, not to her or anyone else.

His teachers always told her he was a bit difficult to get through to. At least that was what the letters home read. She hadn't been able to attend too many parent-teacher conferences on account of her work.

Gregory handled himself pretty well. Hell, he was practically raising himself these days, and why shouldn't he be independent? With his father gone, the household bills fell on her, and she had to put in the hours to make ends meet. They both had to do their part and, to Gregory's credit, he was doing his. He never spoke rudely to her or interrupted her while she worked. He never got suspended from school, nor had any teacher called home with any terrible tales to tell. She was aware of his odd habits and it did bother her that she could not name even one of his friends but, all in all, Gregory was doing all right.

The problem was not with Gregory, she realized, it was with her. Working kept her away from him too much. She missed him and decided she would go start a chat. He could play videogames later. She really only had maybe ten or fifteen minutes to spare anyway before returning to the task of Indiana Electric, but at least it was something. She was about to rise from her chair when a sudden message popped up on her screen. The box containing the message was gray but it had a red header, meaning there was a priority email in her inbox. Those types of messages were uncommon and who would send one at this time of night? Gregory disappeared into the recesses of her mind as she opened the email.

It was her boss in a panic. Something was wrong with the Sanborn Management Report and it had to be fixed and turned in no later than 8 the next morning. Her eyes bulged and a bit of saliva escaped her gaping mouth. A problem with the Sanborn Management Report? That was utterly impossible. She had finished that. It was done!

She had started the Sanborn Management Report at just after 8 that morning. Although, when word of the Avelis Co. and Indiana Electric accounts came her way, she was distracted for a while as she gathered the information needed from various departments within each company, but then she had continued with the Sanborn project.

Then came that nonsense conference call about the issue with the Rodriguez account, which could have been resolved already had the project manager been smarter or actually qualified for her job or at least sober, but after that she had gotten back to the Sanborn project. She had been interrupted with Sanborn again after she had to make a few more calls in regard to the Avelis Co. account, which had set her back further, and then it was time for the second conference call.

That conference call could have ended in disaster as her boss wanted to dump the ECO Properties account on her head. Wanting to be helpful, she had nearly accepted the task when thankfully, Maria, a good friend, stepped up and told her boss that she already was saddled with three others accounts. She owed Maria a big one for that. After that conference call she had finally completed the Sanborn Management Report, emailing it in at around 3 p.m. Sanborn Management was done!

While skimming the email, she saw something about an issue in the accounting spreadsheet, something about wrong numbers, which was entirely impossible. She had entered those numbers right. That was one thing she was sure of and she opened the spreadsheet to prove it. Someone had made a mistake in reading it. Her entry was flawless.

Within a moment however, her eyes welled with tears as her flaws smacked her in the face from the computer screen.

She was partially correct in that she had entered the correct numbers into the spreadsheet. Unfortunately they were one row down and to the left of where they should have been. The spreadsheet was garbage and since the report was based on the spreadsheet, it too was garbage. The entire project would have to be done again. She leaned back in her chair, scrunching her eyes, trying to hold back the tears. She still had to finish with Indiana Electric and now this. It was so late and her eyelids were beginning to angrily force themselves closed.

She leaned forward and sighed, knowing there was no choice. The Indiana Electric report was not due until tomorrow afternoon and would have to be put on the backburner. The remainder of her night belonged to Sanborn Management. She leaned forward in her chair, hunched over her keyboard, and began plugging away at the spreadsheet.

CHAPTER 4

A Fat Kid

The only real exercise that Ronald Pillsner ever got was the 600 foot walk to school. At fifteen, he was a sorry sight: short, pale, and fat. High schools, whether in his home town of North Banfield Wisconsin or anywhere else, were ill-equipped to deal with students like him. Teachers could not always be watching, but other students could. Ronald couldn't run from them, couldn't hide from them, and couldn't fight them. He was just a slow moving target like a slug on the sidewalk being salted a little more each day.

Students were standing near the front door of the

school. Unfortunately, Ronald noticed that Justin and Zach were amongst them. Where Michael was, Ronald didn't know, and that made him nervous. They hadn't noticed him yet, as they were pre-occupied in joking with the girls, making them giggle and squirm. With them there, he couldn't go in the front door. They loved having an audience when they were coming after him. Neither the TV, Internet, or the ancient Roman Coliseum had anything on the live spectacle made out of Ronald on a daily basis.

Ronald hated the girls just as much as he loathed Justin, Zach, and Michael. They'd chastise the boys all while laughing at the show. Those girls adored guys like Justin, Zach, and Michael. They were tall, athletic, and full of confidence. Who wouldn't love them? They had nice hair, flat stomachs, and no male breasts or big bellies to pinch and poke. They had gorgeous names to match their bodies, whereas he was stuck with "Ronald." What kind of name was Ronald anyway? That was the name of the stupid clown who sold burgers and fries that caused people to round out. Like Nikki had said, he was just their toy to amuse themselves with, not a person. A person would never get the kind of treatment Ronald was given.

Ronald didn't know what he would have done without Nikki, his only comfort, well, her and food. Since being contacted online a few months earlier, his days at school might have been hell, but his nights in the bedroom had been thrilling. The cybersex was amazing, and it almost made up for the fact that he'd never get close to a girl. How Ronald wished he could meet her in person, not even for sex, just to say he had one real-life friend. She could finally say the same, too. She was a bully's toy as well, and her life was as meaningless as his. His penis began tightening and he quickly shifted his attention back to Justin and Zach. He didn't need to have a boner spotted.

With the two of them by the front door and so many others around, Ronald needed to become scarce. Around the side of the building, he headed for another door, but just as he reached for the handle, the door swung open and out stepped Michael, tall and buff. With nearly a foot on Ronald, he blocked out the sunlight, leaving Ronald engulfed within his shadow. Michael's hair whipped in the wind as he looked down contemptuously on Ronald like a statue would a gnome.

"I gotta text from Justin saying you were coming around here. You trying to avoid us?" Michael grinned, showing off his pristine pearly whites.

How Ronald hated that smile, no food particles stuck between his teeth, no stains revealing a recent meal. Michael's mouth was just another extension of his perfect body, an attribute which would never need to be bound with braces.

"I'm just trying to get into the school," moaned

Ronald, hearing the approach of the crowd from behind.

"Michael, don't be mean," giggled some bimbo out of Ronald's view.

Michael waved her off and looked back at Ronald, while continuing to sport the same grin, canines leading the way.

"Ronald the Pillsbury doughboy, don't you get it? We've figured out your little plan going in the side of the school. You're kind of hard to miss rolling by the way you do," said Michael.

"Rolling, rolling, rolling, keep that Ronald rolling…"

The mass of, bullies, bimbos, and other rubber neckers boiled over in laughter at Zach's impromptu joke. Zach never missed an opportunity to leach off anything Michael said and claim a small portion of the lime light for himself. To Michael's credit, he didn't seem to mind sharing the stage with his little buddy and often laughed with the crowd.

Attempting to use the laughter as a distraction, Ronald reached for the door again, only to be shoved back by Michael, whose mood had changed on a dime. Gone was the obnoxious jovial bully and out sprang the animal's true essence. Hate spilled from his dark brown eyes and he stepped forward until he was practically standing on top of Ronald. His nostrils flared with rage by the lack of respect Ronald had just shown.

"Where the hell do you think you're going?" snarled

Michael. "Did I dismiss you? Did I say you could go?"

Before Ronald could fathom an answer, Michael gave him a good hard slap to the boobs. It was more than enough to send him to the floor, after which another slap caught him in the face, followed by a swift kick to the side.

"Like that you fat slug? How 'bout it Ronald McDonald? You eat too much of your own food! Roll onto your back. Roll on your back now!"

Ronald shifted into a protective ball, knowing what was coming, but Michael and his size ten-and-a-half shoe rolled him over onto his back. He then gave Ronald a wicked slap to the belly. This one would surely leave a hand print. Justin and Zach stepped up, each slapping his belly a few times each, until Ronald was able to roll over again and begin crawling away. He tried loosing Justin and Zach in the forest of legs that were the crowd, but the forest kept parting, for him and his pursuers. The laughing was the worst part of it and he could never escape it. It reminded him that he was nothing more than a crawling punch line, everyone's favorite joke. It could have gone on forever, but mercifully the bell rang and, as quickly as it started, it ended. Michael, Justin, Zach, and their supporters disappeared into the side door, leaving him alone, on all fours, in the dirt.

CHAPTER 5

A Locker of Vulnerability

After the morning's travesty, Ronald began his daily routine of ducking and weaving down the halls, successfully avoiding everyone for the first two periods. By third period however, he needed to reach his locker for a forgotten book. From around the corner, he peered down the long hallway. It was filled with students who had no interest in him, whatsoever, but Michael, Justin, and Zach's lockers were in the same hallway. Ronald crouched down, trying to stay out of sight. He noticed one of Michael's bimbos walking in the opposite direction. Had she seen him? If she had, she'd probably tell Michael just to get another show. Bimbos loved entertainment.

She disappeared into a classroom and then Ronald made his move. He hated venturing to his locker and tried to do it as seldom as possible. He was completely out in the open, exposed to all with nowhere to run. They had gotten him in the hall before. Sometimes he lucked out and a hall monitor happened by, but other times his books and dignity ended up scattered across the floor.

Going to his locker was a fifty/fifty chance at best. Ronald popped his locker open just in time to feel a double slap from behind on either side of his belly. Justin's slaps stung, but were nothing compared to Michael's, who got him in the belly again as he turned around.

"Pudgy, pudgy, pudgy, pudgy," Michael yelled as he slapped him about the breasts and tummy.

The slaps to his body were bad enough, but even worse was the way his body jiggled after each strike. Like Jell-O, Ronald's flab wobbled and wiggled about, tugging him in every which direction all at once.

After the slaps, Michael grabbed a section of Ronald's stomach and pulled. His pincer-like grip yanked Ronald away from his locker as Justin and Zach threw its contents to the floor. Ronald tore his belly from Michael's grip and, in doing so, stumbled back into Justin and Zach. The three of them clanged into the lockers but did not fall. Instead, Zach reached into Ronald's pants and yanked his underwear. Being extra-large as well as elastic they stretched easily, but by the time Ronald realized what was happening, Zach had attached them to a lower coat hook inside his locker and Justin slammed the door.

With the hallway jeering, Ronald struggled to free himself from the locker but was held in place by his captured underwear. Even worse, the three of them dished out endless rounds of belly slaps, one after another into his soft rolling girth, to the point of nausea. Finally, Ronald's only friend, the bell, rang and once again the crowd dispersed, leaving him to battle for his underwear with his locker.

After a few minutes of struggling, Ronald finally won the war against his locker and got free, although the locker kept a small portion of his underwear as a trophy. Nearly in tears, he sank to the floor and began picking up his books and papers, most of which needed to be returned to his locker. When the late bell rung he was still cleaning up his mess, down on all fours.

CHAPTER 6

A Bully Lunch Chat

T he talk of the lunch table was none other than of Ronald's locker wedgie. Michael, Justin, and Zach received kudos from some of the other boys at their table, and even some of the girls chuckled, too.

"That was kind of funny guys, but it was still mean," said a curly haired girl sitting next to Michael.

"It wasn't mean, it was funny," corrected a boy farther down the table.

"It was really funny," began Michael, pointing to Justin and Zach. "The way you guys got his underwear in his locker was brilliant. I don't think we've ever done that before, and the way he jiggled around trying to get free, I thought I'd die laughing."

"And when you guys hit his belly fat, it made this weird sound, kind of like this 'whoob, whoob, whoob,' sound. It was weird," said a girl sitting next to Zach. She smacked her chewing gum and gave Zach a playful shove.

The jokes shot back and forth across the table, each person trying to outdo the other. One boy said Ronald's lard reminded him of his uncle's pig farm. Another claimed Ronald's stomach had its own zip code.

Zach stated he had actually seen Ronald eat an entire tub of butter, while Justin claimed Ronald had once stolen candy from a baby. The jokes rolled around the table several times over, growing more absurd with each claim, until Michael finally drew everyone's attention back to him.

"You know what I just don't get? I do not understand how Ronald and his fat ass parents keep rolling along. Really, it bugs the hell out of me! My mom was a little overweight, not much and she dies of a heart attack, while Ronald and his porker family are freakin' elephants and they just keep rolling along. It pisses me off that a family of fat garbage like that keeps going. I don't get how their lardo bodies are still living. One thing's for sure, I'll get that little Shamu every chance I get."

"Yeah, that is a good point, Michael. People

shouldn't be lardos like that. I mean does the word 'diet' even exist to them?" asked Zach.

"Really, it's like Ronald doesn't get that I slap him around because he's fat. If he took off the weight, I probably would leave him alone, but why shouldn't I abuse that little turd? Look at 'em," said Michael. "He pisses me off taking up space, waddling around, me having to watch his gut and boobies bounce whenever he moves. Nasty little lard bucket."

"By the way, where is Ronald? Isn't he in this lunch period?" asked Justin.

"I'm not sure if he is or not," said Michael. "He might be, although I'll bet he's hiding somewhere. That's kind of his thing. Remember, he tried to get in the side door this morning. He's around and we'll get him in gym. I have an idea."

Justin and Zach leaned into Michael as he let them in on his little plan. Getting at Ronald in the gym locker room was a national pastime, but they'd have to move quickly, as somehow that little pig often evaded them. Ronald had no business taking up space in a gym class, anyhow, a fact that the entire table agreed on. Once Michael finished explaining his simple plan and what he aimed to do, smiles and laughs once again rolled around the table.

CHAPTER 7

The Library Fortress

During his sixth period lunch, Ronald went to his safe place, the library. He could never navigate the lunch room. Everyone was there and, besides, he had nobody to sit with anyway. Although not technically allowed to eat in the library, if he kept his lunch in his backpack and snuck bites while the librarians weren't looking, he was able to eat in relative peace. It was a bit unnerving having to constantly watch for the librarians and time his chewing just right so they wouldn't get suspicious, but at least it was safe and quiet. Nobody would hassle him while the librarians were looking, plus the fact that from his vantage point, he could clearly observe all three of the entrances to the library.

On one occasion, Michael, Justin, and Zach had entered, maybe seeking him, maybe not, but he was able to escape another way before they ever saw him. They might have learned about his entering the school through the side door, but they knew nothing about the library. That was his guarded secret. When he entered at lunch time he always looked over both shoulders and never used the same entrance every day. That would be too obvious. He also chose different spots to sit within the library as well, chosen for their views of the entrances as well as easy hiding should the need arise.

Ronald's lunch was always large and it took a while to eat, especially while hiding. Although he could see all three of the entrances, because of the library's somewhat triangular configuration, he always had to swivel in his seat to observe at least one of them while being mindful of the librarians, who tolerated no eating. Care had to be taken not to be surprised from behind as well as not to be seen with food from in front. Usually, Ronald did homework or pretended to, in order make his everyday library visits explainable.

When the screaming bell announced the end of sixth period, he always lamented the end of his safe time. He wished he could remain hidden in the peace and tranquility of the library all day, but he couldn't. He had tried it once. The librarian had ordered him to his next class and, to his horror, made a remark about a mustard smell coming from his backpack. He denied eating, and she reiterated that food was prohibited in the library. Ronald immediately complied, not wanting to risk his hiding spot. That had been a frightening moment, as there was no backup plan if he lost the library.

Seventh period would be hell. It was the class fat kids dreaded the most, and the one they could never escape. With his head hanging low, Ronald dragged himself out of the library and headed for his electric chair, his last appeal denied.

CHAPTER 8

The Seventh Period of Hell

For Ronald, going from his sixth period library lunch room to his seventh period gym class was similar to a fat gazelle walking into a lion's den: the locker room. He could claim one advantage over Michael and his cohorts however: distance. It was a very short walk from the library to the locker room, while it was far longer from the actual cafeteria. Ronald estimated that close to 90% of the time, if he was quick enough, he could get into the locker room, change, and escape to the main gym before they arrived. There was, however, the issue of the other 10% of the time.

Upon entering the locker room, Ronald nearly collided with Zach, who shoved him into the lockers. He wasn't sure how Zach had beaten him there, but it meant the other two were lurking somewhere. There were ample places to hide in the locker room jungle and, around every row of lockers, an ambush waited. Michael and Justin could lay low and then move in for the kill when it suited them. One thing Ronald knew was that Zach wasn't there by himself. They operated in a pride and a mauling was inevitable. A little voice deep in the pit of his stomach screamed for him to flee the locker room, flee the school. The voice begged him to run home as fast has his chubby legs would allow and hide in his room. Ronald ignored the little voice, not wanting to get in trouble for skipping a class. He would come to regret his decision, however, as there are far worse kinds of trouble than the kind for cutting class.

Michael and Justin were hidden behind the shower room wall just out of Ronald's view. They were a bit annoyed at Zach for ruining the surprise, but perhaps the plan could still work.

They had snuck out of the lunch room five minutes early, and Michael was determined to get Ronald good, considering the risk he took.

His eyes fixed on Ronald at his gym locker and he crouched down slowly, knowing Ronald might see movement in the dull locker room light. Stalking was almost as satisfying as pouncing, waiting as the excitement built up, ready to climax.

Just as Ronald had his pants around his ankles, Michael leapt from hiding and rammed him with his shoulder. Ronald teetered on his pants-bound feet a moment before plummeting to the floor. He reached down, trying to pull his pants back up and flee, but Michael gave him a hard slap to the face with his big right paw. Before Michael could do anything else, Justin reached into Ronald's locker and pulled out an enormous bag of potato chips. Oh how Ronald regretted putting them in there, but he had run out of room in his regular locker. Michael snatched it from Justin and helped himself to a huge handful of chips.

"Great, now my hands are greasy." Michael bent over and wiped his hands all over Ronald's face, smearing the grease around his chubby cheeks.

From the floor, Ronald tried to resist but another quick slap upside the head ended his protests. After greasing Ronald's face, Michael dumped the remaining chips over his head and walked away, highly satisfied.

The locker room emptied into the gym and Ronald was left alone. He cursed himself for having left the chips in the locker. How stupid could he be? Had he really thought they'd never find the chips? Ronald pulled up his pants, ignoring the potato chips that had found their way into his underwear. Using his gym shirt, he wiped as much of the potato chip grease from his face as he could and then threw it to the ground. God, he hated life!

"Ronald, what is this?"

With his arms folded, one of the gym teachers looked down on him. The teacher motioned to the chips on the floor and gave Ronald an irritated quizzing look.

"Look, Ronald, you need to clean this up. Your gym locker is not your personal refrigerator. When you're at home you can fill all your refrigerators with anything you like, but not in school. You hear me?"

"Well, yeah, but I didn't dump them. I—"

"Ronald, don't start, they are on the floor and I know there're yours. Now hurry up, clean up your mess and get out to the gym."

Without waiting for a reply, the gym teacher stormed off, another school henchman maintaining the status quo and caring only for order and neatness. Ronald decided that he was not going to clean them up. Yeah, they were his, at least they used to be, but he hadn't dumped them. He hadn't made the mess.

Ronald looked to where the teacher had exited "You clean it up," he said. He wouldn't clean it up. He wouldn't. He *wouldn't*!

He wiped his eyes as the cracked and fragile dam began crumbling. Oh God, he thought, he couldn't cry in school. It was all he had left. Nobody had ever seen him cry. He did it all the time from the safety of his bedroom, but not in school. He rushed to the sink and splashed his face with cold water before stepping into the toilet stall.

He had to get out of there, and there was only one way to do it. It would be painful and disgusting, but he had only one out. Ronald took a deep breath, opened his mouth, and stuffed a finger down his throat. In an instant, a wave of food and bile greeted the world and soiled the toilet. Ronald hacked a few times and brought up a second smaller helping of his lunch, followed by several dry heaves. In a matter of seconds, it was over, and he had his out.

ॐ

During the course of the gym class, Michael, Justin, and Zach learned through the grapevine that Ronald had barfed and went home sick.

Michael thought it was funny and hoped he'd lose a bit of weight by puking.

Justin more or less agreed with Michael, but after class was over and the three were back in the locker room changing, Zach began wavering.

"I don't mind pushing the little lardo around some, but he got sick today. I don't want to get in trouble for that."

"Relax, Zach," Justin said. "He'll be stuffing chips down his throat again in no time. Besides, it may not have been us who made him sick. You know how much he eats."

"Well, I still don't like it," Zach said. "I am not getting in trouble for his puking."

"You know, Zach, it almost seems like you feel bad for the little fatty," Michael said.

"I do not. I said I didn't want to get in trouble," Zach yelled. "I don't care about him."

"I hope not, Zach, I hope you don't care about him." Michael glared at Zach until the lackey blinked and laughed at his silly momentary concern.

"You're right, Michael, I won't get in trouble, none at all, and that was what I was worried about. Not him or his puking."

Michael nodded in approval at Zach's righting himself. Fat boy wasn't about to tell anyone about anything. Nobody ever snitched, no matter how bad things were. Fat boy Ronald would just go home and stuff his face to make himself feel better. He'd gain a few more pounds, which would then be slapped around. That was the natural order of things, and Michael had to admit, he liked that order very much.

CHAPTER 9

A Duffle Bag of Feeling

Ronald told the idiot gym teacher about having been sick and, seeing how pale he was plus the stench of his breath, the gym teacher happily sent him to the nurse, who in turn called his mother. Since Ronald lived so close to the school, his mother okayed him walking home. He arrived home in record time, scooted up to his room, and found the large red duffle bag located in the back of his closet.

When he unzipped the bag, he found his joy: Doritos, potato chips, Snickers, beef jerky, Pop Tarts, fruit pies, soda, Twinkies, Hohos, Twix's, cupcakes, Taffy, Cheese

Doodles, Rolo, Gardettos, doughnuts, Butter Fingers, Malomars, Fritos, M&Ms, Skittles, Gummy Bears, cookies, Sun Chips, Reese's Peanut Butter Cups, Milky Ways, Potato Skins, Twizzlers, Cheese Puffs, Corn Chips, Junior Mints, Tootsie Rolls, and marshmallows.

For the next hour he gorged, not stopping for anything save ripping the wrapper off the next treat, barely seeing what was going down the hatch next. The flavors combined into a salty sweet orgy—sex of the mouth. The tears flowed freely from his eyes as the food burrowed toward his stomach. He wailed, he chewed, he sobbed, he swallowed, he cursed, he smacked, he pounded the wall, and he licked his lips. He stuffed himself until he keeled over in exhaustion, finally succumbing to the sugar high, and drifted off into ecstasy.

CHAPTER 10

The Tree and the Distance the Apple Fell

R onald awoke around six in the evening to chocolate stained teeth, an exhausted tongue, and an
outraged stomach. His parents were home. He
could hear the television blasting from the living room.
He nearly stumbled as he rose from the floor, practically
having to pry his tear dried eyes open. After placing his
duffle bag and what was left of its contents back into the
closet, he slowly waddled toward the stairs. His stomach
was pissed, having been so badly abused that day. In the
living room, his parents were parked on the sofa, staring
into the TV. Between the two of them sat a large vat of

buttered popcorn which was continuously washed down with ice cold soda.

"Hi, Ronald honey," chirped his mother. "Are you feeling better?"

"I guess," Ronald said.

None of the four eyes inhabiting his parent's heads ever abandoned the TV. How could they? *The Bachelor* or *Dancing With the Stars* or some other important show was on. Reality TV or their son's reality, how could Ronald compete?

"It was a bad day in school today, Mom," he squeaked.

"I know, honey, I know. The nurse said you got sick. I figured you were sleeping, so I didn't want to wake you. If you're hungry, there is still some calzone left in the fridge, also ice cream for dessert."

"Nah, I ate the last of that," belched his father.

Ronald's father took a swig of soda as he spoke, a drop of which rolled down his first two chins, but was wiped away before reaching the third.

"Why did you finish the ice cream? Ronald might have wanted some," Ronald's mother scolded.

"He got sick. I figured he wouldn't want any. Listen, Ronnie, I know it's tempting to woof down your food fast, but you need to slow down. You've had these vomiting spells before and I think that's the reason. You need to slow it down a little. Food doesn't run away. It's not healthy to keep bringing your lunch back up. It's not good for your body and, well, who knows? The other kids might learn about it and give you a hard time. You don't want that, Ronnie."

"Yeah, I know the vomiting isn't good, Dad," Ronald said, still trying to pry his parent's eyes from the television. "Can I talk to you about school?" he asked.

"A little later, Ronnie," his mother said. "The show is back from commercial."

Ronald started back up the stairs, catching a glimpse of his mother stuffing a handful of popcorn into her mouth. Later wasn't coming. They would watch reality shows until 10 p.m., shower, and then go to bed. At 6 in the morning they would rise, eat a cheese omelet, bacon, hash browns, and toast breakfast, and then be off to work in their office cubicles.

After eight hours of abusing their desk chairs at work, they would come home, eat an eleven-course dinner and watch primetime reality TV. His parents were creatures of habit and later did not exist, just an eternal circle of eating, office work, television, and being as sedentary as possible.

Thankfully, Ronald had one refuge. A few months ago, a girl named Nikki found him in an online chat room.

She too was an outcast and at least she listened. How many times had she saved him from gorging? Ronald sighed, knowing she'd be upset about today's incident. Still he had to be honest with her. After a terrible day in school, she would be there for him. He closed his bedroom door, slumped into his computer chair, and hoped she'd be online.

CHAPTER 11

Ronald and Nikki

*L*ogging onto Automatic Chatting Utility…
Welcome to ACU

77Hercules77: *Hi Nikki, can u talk*

TheGorgeousOne: *Of course Ronald how r u*

77Hercules77: *terrible, had a bad day at school, also gotta tell you something, you'll be mad*

TheGorgeousOne: *What is it?*

77Hercules77: *I did it again I made myself barf so I could go home and then I ate A LOT.*

TheGorgeousOne: *Ronald you know how I feel when you do this.*

77Hercules77: *Are you mad at me? Pleazz don't be.*

TheGorgeousOne: *I'm not mad, I'm upset I care too much about you for you to hurt yourself*

77Hercules77: *I wont do it again I promise*

TheGorgeousOne: *You've said that before, before you do this I want you to at least see if Im online. I'll talk you through this.*

77Hercules77: *ok I will, I don't want you to be mad.*

TheGorgeousOne: *I'm not mad Ronald, tell me about today. Was it Michael and his friends?*

77Hercules77: *yeah, like always, slapping me, pushing me. That whole thing.*

TheGorgeousOne: *They are evil boys*

77Hercules77: *They deserve to die. My dad has a gun, I know the combo to the case. Its my moms birthday*

TheGorgeousOne: *They'll pay eventually, but it isn't time yet. Be patient.*

77Hercules77: *Everbody else laughs at me I cant do anything*

TheGorgeousOne: *In the short term brawn will always beat brains, but not in the long run and we have brains.*

77Hercules77: *yeah, lets see how strong they are when I blow there heads off.*

77Hercules77: *I tried telling my parents but they don't listen*

TheGorgeousOne: *they never do and they can't understand, but I'll listen*

77Hercules77: *I would have killed myself already if i didn't have you. I want revenge I want them dead and I don't care if I die too. I hate my life*

TheGorgeousOne: *Pleazz be calm Ronnie sweety our time will come*

77Hercules77: *There time will come too, Nikki how do you think it'll feel when I blow there heads off?*

TheGorgeousOne: *It will be ecstasy Ronald. You'll feel joy as you fire bullets into them and justice will be served.*

77Hercules77: *Yeah justice. There tougher than me without a gun but not with it.*

TheGorgeousOne: *Guns are the great equalizer, everyone is equal with a gun*

77Hercules77: *even us?*

TheGorgeousOne: *even us*

TheGorgeousOne: *Very soon we'll strike back but it is not time yet. I want U to be calm and strong. Can you do that?*

77Hercules77: *I guess so, I wanna make you happy*

TheGorgeousOne: *You always do sweetie and thats why I cant have you hurting yourself. Your very important to me.*

77Hercules77: *Youre important to me too.*

TheGorgeousOne: *I have to get off now to do some things. Will you be all right?*

77Hercules77: *yeah I guess*

TheGorgeousOne: *ok g'night sweety*

TheGorgeousOne is offline

CHAPTER 12

Wesley and Nikki

*L*ogging onto Automatic Chatting Utility...
Welcome to ACU

Fi$tofCa$h: *Nikki I really need to talk, you there?*

TheGorgeousOne: *Of course sweety how are U?*

Fi$tofCa$h: *bad I wanna die*

TheGorgeousOne: *I get upset when you say things like that. Do u want to make me upset?*

Fi$tofCa$h: *no no, Im sorry*

TheGorgeousOne: *If you are upset talk to me I'm here*

Fi$tofCa$h: *Not happy, I got beat up today, my parents don't care, my dad is drunk*

TheGorgeousOne: *I know being poor is hard*

Fi$tofCa$h: *not just poor, I'm alone, cept you*

TheGorgeousOne: *Always remember you have me, don't forget that.*

Fi$tofCa$h: *I'm tired of being just trailer trash from South Carolina. When am I gonna get my shot?*

TheGorgeousOne: *You'll get your shot…at everyone who hurt you. Remember our time is coming. I promised that.*

Fi$tofCa$h: *I got the guns all right, all over the trailer*

TheGorgeousOne: *Soon we'll put them to use, what did those awful boys do to you today?*

Fi$tofCa$h: *same ole same ole, throw dirt at me, call me names that kinda thing*

TheGorgeousOne: *just awful, youre a nice boy not some trailer trash redneck hick. Nice boys deserve better.*

Fi$tofCa$h: *I wish I had money, but nobody ever did in my family.*

TheGorgeousOne: *what you don't have in money you make up for in decency. That means something to me.*

Fi$tofCa$h: *Thanks Nikki youre the best. I'm so mad at everyone in school. I can't help anything, why can't they just leave me alone.*

TheGorgeousOne: *they can't leave you alone sweety,*

like a pack of wolves they seek out someone to eat. Awful evil boys.

Fi$tofCa$h: *Yeah I'll get them. When can I get them Nikki, just gimme the word and I'll get em good.*

TheGorgeousOne: *Soon sweety soon, we're not quite there yet. Please be patient.*

Fi$tofCa$h: *I am patient but I want em so bad I wanna see there bodys on the ground dead.*

TheGorgeousOne: *PLeazz sweety our time is coming...soon. You want justice be patient, listen to me and you will have it.*

Fi$tofCa$h: *I'll always listen to you Nikki. You're the best girl in the world.*

TheGorgeousOne: *Oh no I'm not, but I care deeply for you and I'm only looking out for you.*

Fi$tofCa$h: *I know Nikki, lifes just too hard and not fair*

TheGorgeousOne: *I know, but soon we'll turn everything upside down.*

Fi$tofCa$h: *yeah!*

TheGorgeousOne: *Ok now I need to get off. Will you be ok?*

Fi$tofCa$h: *yeah I'm good, I love talking to you.*

TheGorgeousOne: *I love talking to you too*

TheGorgeousOne is offline

CHAPTER 13

The Poor Kid

Wesley Brock logged off his library computer and rubbed his bloodshot eyes. He had stayed online too long again. Since he didn't have a computer at home, going to the library was his only option. He chose the one in the back corner, which enabled him to keep his back to the wall, preventing anyone from sneaking up from behind and reading his screen. It was the most privacy he could get anywhere.

He left the library and started the long walk home along the dirt road. He was so tired he hardly noticed the tearing soles of his shoes clap as he walked. Knowing he would wear the same T-shirt and torn faded blue jeans to school tomorrow, he tried his best to slap off the dust kicked up from the road, but it was hopeless. It was even in his scraggily dirty-blond hair. He was just a walking dirt pile.

After a twenty- minute meander, he arrived back at his trailer park. Even before entering his hovel, the smell of tobacco fused with alcohol offended his nose. Apparently his two younger sisters, Kylie and Heaven, had felt the same way and were outside huddled up under a blanket in the hammock. It was a decent enough night to spend outside, though Wesley thought he saw Kylie shiver.

He entered into the living room to see his younger brothers, Luke and Eddie, parked in front of the television, staring at their wrestling program. His father was asleep on the sofa with a beer still in his hand. He snored and spilled a bit on his crotch, but didn't stir. It hardly mattered. He had been out of work for over a year. Nobody seemed to have any need for a second-rate handyman. Across the living room at the kitchen table, sat his mother. She was turned away and Wesley could only see the back of her matted haired head. The ash tray beside her was stuffed with cigarette butts. A fresh one was in her hand and an empty carton sat to the side.

She was reading something, probably some cheap grocery store romance paperback about good-looking people doing it. Wesley thought of going over to talk with her, but even from behind, it was obvious she was engrossed in her book. He turned and started down the short hallway. He briefly looked in on his infant brother Jeff and, from the smell, figured he had soiled himself and most likely had been laying in his filth for some time. The infant was tough though, unlike him, and was accustomed to such trials.

Wesley entered the bedroom he shared with his two younger brothers and collapsed onto the bed. At fifteen, he was the oldest of six. Luckily, little was expected of him in terms of caring for his younger siblings. In the morning, his mother would dump cereal for the little ones and then hotdogs at dinner. His siblings at least had friends in school and sometimes got to eat over at their houses, where they ate chicken and pizza. Wesley rubbed his rumbling stomach, wishing he hadn't thought of food, and then peered under the bed for his prized possessions, his magazines.

He had magazines of all types, all genres, and all products. Whenever he could get his hands on a new one, he leapt at the chance. A waiting room coffee table, a neighbor's mailbox, a trash can, it didn't matter where he got it or what was in it. Every magazine contained the things he loved to look at, dream about, and crave. All of them contained things like Ipods, flat screen televisions, computers, cd players, Ipads, XBOX, comfortable mattresses, boats, grills, sports cars, cell phones, skis, snow-boards, DVDS, Go Carts, laptops, SUVS, motorcycles, jet skis, couches, game cube, fishing gear, RVs, even mansions, aquariums, helicopters, private jets, golf clubs, vacations around the world, tool sets, exercise equipment, snow mobiles, fine dining, brand-name clothing, sporting equipment, shoes, and women. He wanted it all.

Wesley lay back on his bed and closed his eyes. In an instant, he was surrounded by all the goodies of his hoarded magazines. He had money, power, and friends and, for a moment, reality vanished. Gone were the drunken bum of a father and rotting chimney of a mother, gone were his siblings and the bullies, gone was the trail-er and the lives that existed within. Though it lurked in the background of his fantasy, for a moment he was hap-py, blissful, and in ecstasy.

CHAPTER 14

The Ashtray

Wesley's mother had heard her oldest son enter the trailer but was too engrossed in her paperback to acknowledge him. It was a marvelous tale, one of the best books she'd ever found on the pharmacy book rack. The beautiful blonde heroine "Valentina" was forced to make a painful choice between two men competing for her love. Midway through the book, Valentina was leaning toward "Prince Lucas," heir to the throne of all Lusitania. With his great wealth, fine looks, and wonderful locks of hair, he was close to stealing Valentina's heart. Wesley's mom knew, however, that while down, the pirate scoundrel "Captain Vance" the "Vandal of the Seven Seas" was not out. He was dark, tortured, and used his piercing blue eyes to hypnotize his prey. Captain Vance was not beaten yet. He desired Valentina's heart and would stop at nothing to get it.

Wesley's mother had just passed the point where Captain Vance had slain one of Prince Lucas's bodyguards, while Valentina cringed in aroused horror, awaiting her fate at the hands of the Vandal. Wesley's mom nearly fell off her chair in anticipation.

She lit another cigarette and admired the portrait on the book cover. It showed Valentina nearly swooning in Prince Lucas's deep embrace. Her low cut dress barely contained her ample bosom, while her hand reached up and caressed Lucas's impressive mane. In the background, however, Captain Vance stalked, with his long black hair partly hiding his face. His right hand was hidden within his cloak as if drawing a sword. Wesley's mother patted her own tangled, mop-like hair and grinned at the cover, knowing a final showdown between them over Valentina was inevitable.

She put the book down for a moment and sighed, figuring it must be nice having two dashing men fight over you. She looked at her snorting husband on the couch, catching an eyeful of his belly protruding from his stained "wife beater" undershirt. His abs were hidden beneath years of booze and his hair had mostly washed down the shower drain. Since being out of work, the sofa had served as his bed, kitchen table, and on more than one occasion while drunk, his bathroom.

It was lucky for her that she had a job as a reception-ist at a plumbing company or they probably would have lost the trailer months ago. She sat at a desk most of the day, answering phones. Whenever someone would call, she'd put down whatever romance she was in the middle of, roll her eyes, and say "Jed Allan Plumbing. How may I help you?" Then she'd hear a little sob story about a shower stopped up with hair, a sink with a burst pipe, or her favorite, an overflowing toilet some kid had flushed an "Elmo" doll down. All day, every day, she listened to people's plumbing problems.

A few months back, she had tried to get her husband a job with Jed Allan Plumbing, but when Mr. Allan inter-viewed her husband, he politely declined offering a job to him. Her husband knew plumbing, but he showed up to the interview wearing his wife beater shirt and old, torn jeans. He then stumbled over absolutely nothing and knocked over the "Employee of the Month" bulletin board. Mr. Allan could not be sure, but suspected that her husband was drunk. That had been the last "job inter-view" he had done. Now, he was hard at work keeping the sofa occupied and warm. She had to admit that he left an impression on it.

A sleeping belch forced her to turn her gaze to the

two little boys in front of the tube. Her private time was their Wrestling program time. Both wanted to be professional wrestlers, and at one point Wesley did too. She would love for it to happen, as they were well paid, but she doubted it would be possible. All her children were small, scrawny even, but she couldn't figure out why. Her husband was a big, hulking man and she certainly was not shopping in the petit section either, yet her children were undersized. She pondered the question as she turned in her seat and lit a fresh cigarette.

Oh well, she thought. Her children were all right, even if they were on the small side. They had a good diet of hotdogs and pasta most of the time, and they stayed away from their father's booze. The TV and the school did most of the work in raising them and that more than made up for their lack of a father. She put the thought of her children aside, flicked a bit of ash off the end of the cigarette, and reopened her book. Now where was she? Oh yes, Captain Vance had killed one of Prince Lucas's men. How could she forget?

CHAPTER 15

Proper Gregory in School

Most human beings, kids and adults alike, simply stepped off the bus when the door opened. Gregory, however, was unlike most other human beings. Before stepping off the bus, his proper ritual of stamping his feet three times each on the last step had to be performed. It was a ritual that left everyone behind him perturbed and many had no issue about expressing their irritation.

"Come on, spazz, we don't have all day."

Gregory ignored the student behind him, accustomed to the abuse. He completed the required stamping and, only then, stepped off the bus. He heard the comments of "spazz," "retard," "weirdo," and others, but none of that fazed him in the slightest. At age sixteen, he had learned to cope with a life of no friend. Most of the comments came from students who otherwise simply ignored him. He didn't need friendships anyway. They only got in the way of doing things properly. He just needed to be left alone and most of the students in school could be counted on for that.

There were others, however, others he had to be careful of, others who actively sought him out, looking to punish him for doing things in the proper way. Ducking down behind a tree like a soldier, he scanned the vicinity for the others. If he could locate them first, he could avoid them all together. Avoidance was the proper way of dealing with them. They attacked in a pack. That was their proper way of doing things, and Gregory had to admit that it was very effective.

Oblivious to the stares of bewildered students, he crept toward the entrance of the school. While aware of his fellow students, Gregory was keeping watch for the Pack. They stalked somewhere. They were hunters with traps everywhere, always trying to ensnare him. At times he'd fall into their traps, but he could also escape and evade. Every day was a new game.

Success, he made it into school undetected. He then cast a wary eye around a corner, down the hall. There they were. The Pack was standing by his locker, expecting him to come along at any moment. Gregory smirked to himself, baffled that they could actually be so stupid. *They're getting sloppy*, he thought.

Gregory had long ago figured out how to avoid using his locker. Oh, at one point their presence by his locker drove him mad, but he was cunning and now no longer needed to visit it. *Let them have it,* he thought, and started down the opposite hall.

"Where the hell is he? Simon asked. "I'm bored."

"Shut up, Simon," Ray said. "That spaz will be coming along any minute. He has to get into his locker."

"He might see us waiting here," said Caleb.

"He might, but who cares? He's due for a treatment, if you know what I mean," Ray said.

Simon, Caleb, Garrett, and Eric all knew exactly what Ray meant. They smiled in anticipation of the good show that was coming. All except Eric, who stood stoically.

He didn't like Gregory, but thought the treatments were a little harsh. He also worried about hurting Gregory and getting into trouble. If he got in trouble, his parents would have at him.

"Maybe we shouldn't do any treatment…you know, maybe just throw his books around the hall?" Eric said.

"Eric, quit being a pussy, all right? Gregory needs his treatments," Ray said.

"Really, Eric, why do you feel sorry for him? He's a spaz. Who cares? Hey, Ray, do a good hard one today," Simon said.

"Oh, I will," Ray replied.

"I'm just worried about really hurting him with those treatments. We could get in trouble," said Eric.

Ray sneered. "If you're so worried about your spazzy boyfriend, then why don't you go find him and warn him? Eric, you can piss off."

"Never mind, fine, whatever," Eric said.

He leaned back against the lockers and looked toward Garrett for support that wasn't coming. Garrett just stood by and quietly laughed when Simon and Caleb did. Every time Ray cracked a joke and Simon and Caleb broke out giggling, then so did Garrett. When they stopped, so did Garrett. It wasn't often you saw two human beings share a shadow.

"Hey, Garrett, I'll bet Gregory is hiding outside. Go out there and look," ordered Ray.

Without a word Garrett raced toward the door. He was gone for several minutes before running back, shaking his head. He hadn't found Gregory.

"Where the hell is he hiding?" asked Caleb

"Who knows, we'll get him later. Right now we gotta get to class. Let's go."

On Ray's command the Pack traipsed down the hall away from Gregory's locker. They missed him that morning but the day was still young with plenty of time for a treatment.

⁊с⁊

Gregory had slipped away and found his favorite bathroom, the one next to the woodshop lab, the one that other students rarely ever used because it was so far out of the way. He smiled at his cunning as he crossed the threshold right foot first. After making sure it was empty, he entered the handicapped stall at the far end. He stood on the toilet and then stepped up onto the safety bar. This added height gave Gregory the ability to reach the soft tiled ceiling. His balance was precarious, but he gently moved one of the ceiling tiles and pulled two stashed books from the ceiling. He then stepped down and exited the bathroom, looking both ways before starting down the hall. Everything had gone right that morning. Now he wouldn't have to worry about the Pack until fifth period. He congratulated himself as he victoriously strode toward his first class.

From careful surveillance, Gregory knew that the Pack had their first two period classes on the other side of the school, while his first and second periods were located in the same hall. Sure, he'd have to face them eventually, but for now he could move freely down the hallway with only whispers, stares, and minor taunts. Even so, he was always on alert as any one of the students to his left or right could be a Pack informant. It was important to remain on guard at all times and never allow anyone to sneak up on him.

When walking, Gregory tended to hunker down and move his head from side to side. The purpose of this was perfectly obvious. He kept low in order to avoid flying objects, which people often chucked at him, and he swiveled his head from side to side in order to better scan the entire hallway. That was how one maintained a properly secured walk through a hallway. So close was he to his class, he nearly died of shock when the Pack whirled around a corner and confronted him. They should have been on the other side of the school. Nothing about this encounter was proper! Gregory stepped back, fully aware that this time he had fallen into the trap. Those five nasty boys had somehow gotten the drop on him.

"We missed you at your locker, spazzoid," growled Ray. "Where you hiding?"

He seized Gregory's backpack strap and hurled him into a locker. Gregory grabbed his throbbing shoulder and breathed deeply. It was okay, he thought. He had enough hit points to take the shot. The Pack always tried stealing his hit points. Little did they know that he had developed the ability to regenerate them. Unfortunately, they could still hurt him plenty before regeneration could happen.

Gregory gazed down, unable to look them in the eyes. He could never look them in the eyes. They would drain him, suck his strength, and deplete his hit points. The eyes were far more dangerous than their hands or feet. All eyes were dangerous and all must be avoided, such was the proper way of dealing with others' eyes.

"What are you looking at, spazz? My dick? You lookin' at my dick?" Simon asked.

Gregory wasn't looking at anyone's dick, but the way he bent his gaze made it appear that he might have been.

"No—Simon." Gregory blurted out. "I—I—" This was his weakness. He got flustered in improper situations and then began stuttering. He couldn't do confrontation and the Pack knew it.

"I, I, I, I" mocked Simon. "Man you're such a retard. Why are you so retarded?"

"He was dropped on his head too many times as a baby," Caleb answered.

The Pack laughed at the joke as Gregory tried slipping away, but Ray was not about to miss him a second time.

"Oh no, you don't, spazzoid. You need to have your head examined."

"*No!*" Gregory cried, knowing what was about to happen.

It was the Pack's favorite game, their favorite weapon, one that stripped Gregory of all his hit points.

"Hold him," shouted Ray, as Simon and Caleb each grabbed a shoulder.

In a last ditch effort to escape, Gregory lobbed a kick toward Ray, but it fell short and Ray just laughed. He took a firm grip on either side of Gregory's head and began shaking. Gregory's head was shaken back and forth and the world became nothing more than blurred vision and Pack cackling.

"You need treatment! You need treatment!" *Dr.* Ray yelled.

The treatment continued on and on and only ended when Ray's arms grew tired. Gregory collapsed in a heap, his hit points drained as the Pack walked off. Eric was last in the Pack line. He looked back at Gregory to see if he was okay. Gregory was moving, which Eric interpreted as a sign he was all right and not injured.

When Eric began lagging behind, a quick, "Come on," made him speed up and rejoin the Pack. "See you later, spazzoid."

In his spinning, nauseated state, Gregory couldn't be sure which one had said it, but all order and propriety were gone. He heard the bell, but needed a few minutes on the floor to regain some of the hit points he'd lost. Some would come back after a short time but some were lost forever. A few straggling students stepped over him to get to their classes, but mostly, he was alone.

After sitting idly on the floor for several minutes, he warily rose to his feet and leaned against the lockers. The treatments always left him feeling horribly improper. Ray was a mad scientist.

Little did he or his minions realize the monster they were creating.

Gregory was almost ten minutes late when he stumbled into class.

"Gregory, why are you late? Everyone else arrived on time." The teacher, a mousy, snippy little woman stood at attention with her hands on her hips, expecting an explanation. All she got was a hunching, stuttering boy watching the ground.

"I'm up here, Gregory," she said, pointing to her eyes. "Why don't you ever look people in the face? You're being very rude."

"I—I'm sorry," Gregory stuttered, making small glances toward her face.

From the corner of his eye he could see the smiles of embarrassment, the rolling eyes, and the looks of morbid fascination from the class. Some of the students had undoubtedly seen the examination, but no one talked. Snitching was not the proper way of doing things.

"Just sit down," said the frustrated and clueless teacher, and Gregory did.

From that point until his fifth period lunch was an isolated but peaceful time for Gregory. He was left alone and that was enough for him. Teachers and students alike would tolerate his presence and ignore or simply humor his jerky movements. At least he was left to recoup his lost hit points. He'd need them at lunch.

CHAPTER 16

Pack Chat

The cafeteria was a death trap and both hunters and prey knew it. All the students were required to be in the lunch room until the bell rang and the two worthless lunch room teacher's aids, instead of being on guard, would sit at their own table up front and yak for the entire forty minutes.

Gregory had tried to sit at the table next to them but their eyes burned him. They would relentlessly stare, intent on seeing into his mind. Gregory would not allow that. He was careful not to look them in the eyes, so he only stole glances with his peripheral vision, but finally, he decided he couldn't stay near them and, hence, was on his own at lunch. Generally, he would hide in a back corner where extra chairs were stacked up. He would quickly rearrange them into a small fort with one chair to sit on and another as his lunch table. From this vantage point, he could see the entire cafeteria and no one could sneak up on him. If someone tried an attack on his fortress, he had a secret weapon.

The Pack entered a few minutes after he did and sat down at their regular table. This was expected as they always ate before the hunt. With full bellies their strength would rise, and then they'd be ready. Gregory munched down his own ham and cheese sandwich as he watched them do the same. Every once in a while, they would take peeks in his direction. They were plotting, but Gregory wasn't stupid. This time, he'd see them coming and he had an ace up his sleeve. His plan might not take out all of them but it would neutralize at least one or two and give him a moment to escape. They got him earlier but not this time.

The Pack knew they were being watched. Each of them would peak toward him then look away, laughing. Even Eric could not stop from giggling at the ridiculous kid in the corner fortress who made a castle out of chairs.

"What a screwed up little spazzoid," Caleb said. "And he wonders why we go after him. Duh, I know, because he's a spazzoid."

"Who knows what's wrong with him? I better shake him even harder at his next treatment," Ray said with a smile.

Eric gave Ray a scornful look, but when Ray returned it with interest, Eric immediately gazed back down at his egg salad lunch. It was sort of funny picking on Gregory, but Eric was convinced that the head treatments went too far.

Eventually, Gregory would get hurt and then all hell would rain down on them. Still, Eric was relatively new at this school and these were his friends. He had once tried looking to Garrett for support, but he always hid behind Simon and Caleb.

"You know what?" Simon started. "I'll bet he really was dropped on his head as a baby. I know we say that all the time, but I'll bet it's true."

"Could be," Ray said. "Hey, Garrett, that happened to a cousin of yours, right? Your aunt dropped him on his head and now he's screwed up?

Garrett swallowed his sandwich hard and nodded. That had indeed happened and his cousin still suffered from the effects of that accident. His aunt suffered, too.

"Yeah, Garrett, that's pretty bad, but I'll bet your cousin isn't half as screwed up as Gregory," Ray said.

Simon and Caleb giggled as Garrett chomped down another mouthful of sandwich. He smiled through the food and shook his head.

"Nobody on planet Earth is as screwed up as Gregory," Ray said.

"That's for sure," Caleb said.

"Oh yeah," Simon said.

"Probably true," Eric said.

Garrett nodded.

In fifteen minutes, the Pack had cleared their lunches and began sniffing him out. They rose and started over for the corner. Gregory was careful not to smile. His plan was ready and he didn't want to arouse their suspicions. Eric and Garrett were to the rear of the Pack, out of range for what Gregory had planned. Caleb, while theoretically close enough, was still a long shot, but Ray and Simon were right where he needed them to be.

Ray laughed. "Yo, Greg, I think it's time for another treatment."

With Ray's declaration, Gregory enacted his plan. He placed both hands underneath one of the large stacks of chairs, intent on sending it tumbling down on the lead Pack member. The plan might have worked, if only Gregory hadn't misjudged the weight of more than a dozen stacked chairs. Tipping them took longer than expected and required more force. In this window of time, Ray and the Pack realized his plan and moved out of its path. When the stacked chairs finally did tumble, it did no more damage than make a loud startling clang throughout the cafeteria.

The two yakking teacher's aids heard the commotion and rushed over to see chairs sprawled out all over the floor.

"What's going on?" one of them inquired.

"I don't know," Ray whined. "We were walking over here and Gregory tried knocking the chairs over on us."

The other boys quickly concurred as Gregory sat mesmerized by the ease of their lying.

"Is this true, Gregory?" asked the other aid.

"They—they were coming over," Gregory stammered.

It was the truth, couldn't they see that?

"Knocking chairs over is not acceptable. You could have hurt someone. Let's go, Gregory."

Gregory got up and walked out with the aids. He peered over his shoulder and saw the Pack silently cackling. He had to hand it to them. They weren't stupid. When their initial plan of giving him a treatment failed, they quickly adapted and still ensnared him in another improvised trap. Very clever, thought Gregory. He envied the ease they had in doing things properly, and from their perspective, this was very proper. They failed to hurt him, but still got him into trouble. Gregory wished he could improvise that quickly. It usually took him several agonizing days to adapt. *It's not fair*.

He waited in the principal's office for ten minutes before the man finally walked in. The middle aged, balding, potbellied man eased into his oversized leather chair and wiped the eternal spewing sweat from his forehead. Gregory carefully looked down.

He was in a dangerous place and he could not allow eye contact.

"Now look, Gregory," the principal began dryly. "I know that Ray and Simon and the rest of them can be a bit obnoxious. I also know they have on occasion annoyed you a little bit. I assure you, Gregory, that I am fully aware of all that goes on in this school. Now that all being said, you cannot knock chairs onto them. That could have really hurt someone and I don't think you want that. So, Gregory, can we agree to not allow this little incident continue any further?"

As far as breaks went, Gregory was getting a big one. All he had to do was answer yes and the principal would cease probing his mind. He could feel the principal's reluctant fingers on the outskirts of his consciousness, almost begging him to just say yes so as to spare them from having to enter the dark and gloomy place that was Gregory's thoughts. The principal feared the dark and Gregory feared the light, and a compromise was reached.

"Yeah, I won't do it again—sorry."

Satisfied, the principal smiled and exhaled in relief as Gregory felt the little fingers retreat from his mind. With the possibility of having to continue the conversation with this odd boy averted, he leaned back in his chair and smiled.

"Good. I'll write you a late pass and you can get to your next period."

Before heading for sixth period, Gregory made a stop at his bathroom ceiling locker. All in all, he felt he could just barely declare victory, like a boxer who won on points. The cowardly principal didn't want to deal with him and had let him off easy, plus, he had escaped a head-shaking treatment. The last four periods of the day would be easy enough. Caleb was in one of those classes with him, but he would never attack outside the safety of the Pack. The next trial was after the ninth-period bell. The Pack would surely remember the chair-tipping insult.

The remainder of the day was spent scurrying from class to class, scrutinizing every hallway before starting down it, using shortcuts when possible, and always keeping a sharp eye out for the Pack. He needed this time to continue upping his hit points. There was a battle awaiting Gregory at the end of the day, one that could destroy him. They knew what bus he rode on and, often times, they intercepted him on the way there, but today he had a plan.

Gregory always had a plan and usually they worked pretty well. The chair-tipping fiasco was an aberrant. Usually, his fighting plans were inferior compared to his hiding and avoidance plans. That was where he was an expert. Just the other day, he had come up with a plan on how to reach his bus while avoiding the Pack and it would be all thanks to the bathroom that held his ceiling locker.

When the bell rang at the end of the day, he scampered into his ceiling-locker bathroom, paying no attention to which foot entered first. So intent was he on escaping out the window in the back of the bathroom, that he did not notice that Caleb had quietly followed him into the bathroom and watched him slip out. This revelation was immediately texted to Ray. Caleb grinned. Ray would be so pleased, especially after having missed him that morning at his locker and then again at lunch.

Once outside the window, Gregory crept toward the front of the school where the buses were lined up. His bus driver was as reliable as the sunrise. Every day she would pull up to the school about twenty minutes before the bell then sit in her seat and read. Because of this habit she was almost always first in line in front of the school and, more importantly, it meant a short walk for Gregory from the bathroom window to his bus. Once onboard, Gregory would be safe.

None of the Pack rode his bus. From his position along the wall, his bus was in full view with his portly old driver relaxed in her seat with a book covering her face. Just then, for the second time in a day, the Pack jumped out from around a corner.

"I knew I saw you bolt out the window," Caleb said as Ray patted him on the back.

Gregory silently cursed himself. How could he have been so stupid again? He had not paid attention to which foot he had stepped into the bathroom with first. And now he was going to pay a high price. Then a glimmer of hope emerged. If he could race back to the bathroom, climb through in the window, and enter in the proper manner maybe he could make things right. Before the Pack could say anything more, he turned and ran. It was his only chance. He needed to reenter the bathroom and do things properly. That would set things right. He hadn't urinated so he could still go back.

While Gregory was not the slowest runner in school, he was far from the fastest and, with his backpack bouncing on his shoulders, the Pack had little trouble catching up. Ray was first. He grabbed Gregory's backpack and pulled him to the ground. Once down, the kicks began all over, destroying any chance of getting back to the bathroom and making things proper.

"Geeze, retardo, sneaking out the bathroom window, knocking over chairs, you need another treatment," Ray yelled.

The leader of the Pack reached down to clutch Gregory's head, but the prey lunged up and shoved him. Ray stumbled back a few feet as the kicks from the Pack continued. Gregory tried crawling from the legs but they kept following and when extra hard kicks began striking him, he knew Ray was back. Finally, he curled up into a ball and just protected his head, accepting the fact that the pack had ensnared him and his hit points were gone.

Ray kneeled down on top of him and gave him several swift punches about the head, while Caleb and Simon kicked him in the back. Eric and Garrett cheered from the side, now fully engrossed in the show. With the Pack chanting his name, Ray grabbed either side of Gregory's head and began shaking once again.

"I'm doing this for your own good, spazzoid! One of these days this will make you normal! *Be* normal!" The treatment stopped with the yelling, Ray gave one last kick to the belly before turning to the other Pack members.

"C'mon, we're gonna miss our buses."

Eric looked back again at the pile that was Gregory and shook his head. He could have fought back if he wanted, but he ran. He did deserve this. Ray was right. That spaz deserved every treatment he got. Why did he have to act like that? It was only a game they played anyway. Gregory was all right.

"Fun stuff huh, Garrett?" Ray asked.

Garrett nodded.

The Pack walked off, leaving Gregory a pulp in the grass. The shaking made everything wrong with no way to right it. Or was there some way? Was there still possibly some small way of making things at least a little bit proper? Crawling, Gregory made his way back toward the bathroom window. It seemed much farther than it should have been with each foot crawled feeling like ten, but he had to make it. After several moments of crawling, he pulled himself back through the window into the bathroom. Once inside he struggled to his feet and exited the bathroom door, before turning around and entering right foot first. Things were a little better now, more proper. After making things right in the bathroom, he went back out the window and just sat beneath it. His bus was gone now. He knew that, but it was only a two mile walk home. He would start the walk soon, but for the moment he needed a little time to rest and allow his hit points to recover.

CHAPTER 17

Wesley Broke

W esley tossed his beat-up backpack over his left shoulder. The right shoulder strap had snapped months ago. He eyed the pea-sized hole in his shirt and prayed it wouldn't get any bigger, though only a few days earlier, that pea hole had been a pin hole. He tried wiping away various spots of dirt from his skin, but they were stubborn and it seemed that his skin was stained.

Most of his school was solidly middle class and seemingly unaware that all it would take was one bad break in the family to send them spiraling into poverty.

Yet, they looked down on him. Some referred to him as Wesley Broke, but what did it matter? Broke or Brock, either way, he didn't respond.

Wesley opened his locker, wondering where Scotty and the rest of them were. They'd arrive soon to start in on him as the hallway was void of teachers. *Filthy scumbags*, he thought.

He knew their game. They preferred to start with him when a teacher was nearby but out of earshot, just to see if they could get him in trouble. They succeeded more often than Wesley wanted to admit.

Then his parents would get a call and his father would have to leave his booze behind to come to the school and have at him.

"Hey, Wesley Broke. That a new pair of pants?" There was Scotty, a little late but he showed up.

"Drop dead, Scotty," Wesley replied.

Scotty laughed, ignoring the remark. "Man, you smell bad." He looked at Kyle, Taylor, and Barry for confirmation. "Doesn't he?"

"He stinks something awful," Taylor said. "Kinda like if a skunk burrowed up a horses ass."

The boys howled as Wesley closed his locker. Wesley wasn't a fighter. Being scrawny, he wasn't built for it and neither did he have the temperament. He began walking away, knowing he'd never be allowed to.

"Where're you going, Wesley Broke? You're gonna

spread your stink down the hall," Kyle yelled. "God, Wesley, do you even own a shower?"

Wesley did own a shower but it had been broken the last few days. He had a bit of musk to his scent but didn't reek. Wesley was sure of that as he quickened his pace. They matched his speed and continued taunting and sniffing him all the way down the hall. The last straw was when Kyle put his thumb in the pea sized hole in his shirt and tugged. With unknown strength, Wesley shoved Kyle into a row of lockers, much to the surprise of everyone.

"Wesley!" Before any of the boys could react, a teacher asserted her presence in the hall. She was a woman, who appeared to be about ninety years old but wore too much makeup in an attempt to look a mere seventy. She started toward them, swaying back and forth as she moved. Tall and lean, she towered over many of the students, including Wesley. The journey from her spot to where the boys stood frozen seemed to take an eternity. When her odyssey ended, she waved the other boys away and looked down solely on Wesley.

"Wesley, we do not shove in these hallways," she stated, pointing a boney finger at him.

"They started it!" Wesley exclaimed. "They were telling me I smelled and they made the hole in my shirt bigger."

"Wesley, I don't care about what they were *saying*. I care about what you were *doing*, and you shoved Kyle into the wall. As for that hole in your shirt, I saw that the day before yesterday when you wore that rag to school. Look, Wesley, I know you live in a trailer park and things are…different there, but we do not use violence in this school. Are we clear, Wesley?"

He grimaced up at the old fossil but then nodded. What did she care? She was nothing more than the status quo's keeper. Were all the kids breathing? Yes? Excellent, order has been maintained. What other purpose did she serve? The day would only get worse from there. Scotty and the others would be waiting for him in first period.

Wesley sat on the far side of the classroom near the window, while the four nasty creatures sat in the middle of the room. In spite of the distance between them, they always found a way to get at him. Sometimes, they threw things, while other times, they'd draw pictures of him and pass them around the room, all the while the monotone teacher, two years from retirement, stared at the chalk board droning on about whatever subject he used to care about.

Halfway through class, Taylor began drawing and Wesley could bet the picture was of him. Taylor was a talented artist who used his skill to humiliate him every chance he got. Wesley was so intent on what Taylor was doing that he did not notice what Scotty was up to.

Where Scotty had gotten a straw was anybody's

guess. What he was planning, however, was obvious. Scotty placed a small bit of paper in his mouth. Once moist enough, he placed it in the straw and fired at Wesley. Whether by accident or impeccable design, the slobbered pellet struck inside his ear. Wesley pulled it out and chucked it to the floor, as the creatures celebrated the amazing shot. Wesley barely had time to wipe the spit from his ear when Taylor finished his drawing and passed it to the kid in front of him. Soon it would reach Wesley, but not before most of the class would get a glimpse. Wesley spied the clock, despising its mockingly slow passage of time.

There was no question the day would go on forever. All that kept Wesley going was the knowledge that Nikki would be waiting for him online after school, his angelic saving grace. How he longed for a picture of her, but he hadn't had the courage to ask. He bet she was as gorgeous as her name, a sweet caring soul who plucked lost boys from the darkness and brought them into her loving, caring light. She always knew what was best. She kept him calm when all he wanted to do was burn down the world.

A tap on his shoulder disrupted his daydream of Nikki. The chortling idiot from behind handed him Taylor's drawing and his obvious talent enraged Wesley. Taylor could easily make a decent living doing boardwalk caricatures. The face in the picture was clearly his, only with an exaggerated nose, warped ears, and, of course, the stink lines rising from his disheveled hair. Wesley loathed Taylor and his talent. Why couldn't he draw landscapes or something?

Wesley's eyes met Taylor's and the standoff began. Taylor wanted Wesley to pass the picture along so that the rest of the class could view his work. Wesley wanted to tear it up but the nasty artist looked coldly at him, silently threatening serious consequences if he harmed his artwork. Taylor's fists clenched, his eyes narrowed, and his face turned beat red. Wesley got the message, but this was one of the few times where he had the edge over all four of them. He grinned at Taylor and tore the picture to pieces. Taylor leaned back in his seat, nodding, as Wesley read his thoughts. Oh yes, there would be hell to pay for that. Scotty, Kyle, and Barry quietly egged Taylor on, telling him to teach Wesley the proper respect for art.

Knowing the hellish walk he would face once in the hallway, Wesley quickly packed up before the bell and, the moment it rang, scooted out the door. He came into a bit of luck as Taylor, Scotty, and Kyle got caught up in a bottle-neck at the classroom door, but Barry managed to squeeze through and pursued him down the hall. From behind, he gave Wesley a vicious shove into the lockers, which sent Wesley to the floor. He tried to get up but Barry sat on him and began grabbing Wesley's face with his hands.

"You got no respect for great works of art, stinky."

The other three caught up a moment later and Wesley struggled futilely while looking up at Taylor in horror. In Taylor's hand was a black indelible marker, and Wesley's face was to become his canvas. He almost squirmed away but, at the last moment, Scotty and Kyle grabbed his arms as the marker neared his face.

"I'm gonna draw the stink lines on your face, so that everyone will know that you stink," Taylor giggled as he marked Wesley's face, up and down, left and right, over the eye lids, lips, cheeks, nose, everywhere. "There you go," Taylor exclaimed. "Now you're a work of art."

With the artwork complete, he recapped the marker. The four of them enjoyed a few cheap kicks to Wesley's belly before wandering off down the hall.

Wesley got off the ground and rubbed his face, knowing it would do nothing against the indelible marker. He stumbled into the nearest bathroom, almost in tears, and viewed his blackened face in the mirror. Smeared marker was everywhere and made it appear that he wore black rouge, eye shadow, and lipstick. The few tears that followed did little to clean his violated face.

He scrubbed, using the industrial alcohol-based soap from the dispenser that dried out his skin. Eventually, he was able to get most of the black off, but washing his face, plus rinsing his eyes after burning them with soap, devoured nearly twenty minutes of his next class. Wesley had stumbled into the bathroom black faced and exited red faced which was little better.

The teacher scowled when he walked in. "Well thank you for showing up, Wesley. Now I can tell the office not to look for you anymore."

"It wasn't my fault—" he started.

"Of course not," mocked the teacher. "Being late is never any student's fault."

She impatiently waved him to his seat as she returned to her meaningless lecture. Taylor was the only one of the four in the class with him and he was working double time not to burst from laughter.

Wesley was such a loser, from a loser family, in a loser trailer park, who stunk like dirty clothes left out in the summer sun. It was always fun going after him, plus it gave Taylor a chance to display his artistic talents. He'd always had an eye for color and shadow, although with Wesley all that was needed were black stink lines. Taylor couldn't wait until lunch to gloat about his drawing on Wesley's face with the others. Until then, he'd chuckle quietly and draw more pictures of Wesley Broke.

CHAPTER 18

Laughing at a Marker Face

When Taylor arrived at his table at lunch time, his friends were already waiting for him.

They hadn't had time in the hall, but now the congratulations went around for not only the classroom drawing, but also the facial one.

"You totally turned him into a marker face, Taylor," Kyle said.

Scotty laughed. "Yeah, you actually made him smell worse, with all that marker."

"That was so funny," added Barry.

"That stinking kid needs to learn that you don't rip

up my works of art." Taylor pulled out his large sketch-book and laid it on the table.

It was filled with drawings, a few of Wesley, but mostly other objects such as rooms, plants, cars, things of that nature. The other three boys agreed he was talented but preferred to look at the pictures of Wesley.

"Can I see that one of Wesley with the skunk again?" Kyle asked.

Taylor groaned, wanting to show them some of the non-Wesley drawings he had, but the table had spoken and so he flipped back to the requested picture. It showed Wesley, stink lines and all, in a full kissing embrace with Pepe le Pew from the Looney Tunes.

That's so funny, Taylor," Barry said.

Scotty and Kyle laughed, too. Pepe held Wesley in a deep dip and was kissing him just as deeply. Unlike the little black and white female cat Pepe usually molested who tried in vain to escape, Wesley was drawn to enjoy the embrace and appeared to be nearly in a swoon.

"I gotta tell you, I feel really bad for that skunk," Scotty said.

"That skunk should have Wesley's stink gland re-moved," added Kyle.

"Ha, ha, that's so funny guys," Barry said.

Taylor waited for his friends to finish gawking at the picture. He had other ones to show, good ones, too. He wanted to show the sketch he made of his church. He was especially proud of that one, with the way he caught the shadow of the setting sun. He also wanted to unveil the picture he drew of the little black Corvette he saw in the library parking lot a week earlier. These were works he truly took pride in, not nonsense sketches of dirty ole Wesley.

"Hey guys," Taylor started. "Look at this one right here." He flipped in his sketchbook to the drawing of the church. He expected to leave his friends in awe but all he got were a few nods.

"Yeah, that's great, Taylor," Scotty said. "I like how you colored inside the lines on that one. Go back to the skunk and stinky."

"Ha, ha, that's funny, Scotty," Barry said.

"Hey, wait a second, Scotty, art is more than just lines," Taylor said. "There is a lot of technique to it. I'm hoping to major in it in college."

Scotty giggled. "Oh, yeah, Taylor, for sure. Techniques like 'Should I use a green crayon or a blue crayon?'"

"That's so funny, Scotty," Barry said.

"It's more than that and you know it, Scotty," Taylor fired. "In college, they really go into stuff like this, especially if you major in art."

"When I'm in college, I'm going to major in booze and minor in pussy," Scotty said.

Kyle and Barry rolled at the joke as Taylor shoved

his sketchbook into his backpack, returned to his lunch, and waited for Scotty to stop laughing.

"Hey, Taylor, maybe you can draw a picture of beer and a pussy," Scotty said. "Then we can combine majors."

"That's so funny, Scotty," Barry said.

Taylor ignored the comment and continued waiting out the three stooges' laughter. They couldn't get art, all they saw were lines and colors. They lacked the maturity he possessed and Taylor had to admit to himself that sometimes he got weary of having to dumb himself down for the three of them. They were typical silly teenage boys, whereas he was intellectually much older, gifted even. While they viewed "pussy" on the internet, he studied the curves and structure of women. While they gawked over amazing cars in magazines, he saw the styling genius of their designers. While they saw only a sun set, he viewed God's artwork in the sky. These boys were beneath him.

A moment later Scotty and Kyle rose from their seats and walked over to some girls on the other side of the lunch room, leaving Taylor and Barry alone.

"Art is more than just lines and colors, Barry. You know that, right?" asked Taylor.

"Oh, sure," Barry said.

"There is a lot of time and focus that goes into works of art," Taylor continued.

"Sure, yeah," Barry said."

"Scotty should respect art a little more, right?"

"I guess."

Barry shrugged and took a big bite of his banana while scratching his head. Taylor watched Barry as he ate, thinking that all he needed to do was take him and put him in a tree. Taylor and Barry sat quietly for a few minutes until Scotty and Kyle returned. The fact that Barry lit up when Scotty sat down beside him wasn't lost on Taylor. Every day when he got home from school, his Golden Retriever, Leo, would look at him in much the same way, and he had the sketches of Leo to prove it.

"Hey guys," Scotty started, "I was just told that Wesley is out in the hall on a bench, right now. Probably stinking it up bad."

"We should go out there so Taylor can draw another picture of him, unless he just wants to draw a building, or table, or maybe a piece of bird crap," Kyle remarked.

"That's so funny," Barry said.

"N—no, I—I can draw him again," Taylor stammered.

"I don't know, Taylor," Scotty said. "You seem kinda busy with your art techniques and all that crap."

"Yeah," Kyle added. "He needs to work on his technique."

"Up yours, Kyle," Taylor said. "I have an idea of what I can do to him to piss him off."

"What?" Scotty asked. "Draw him with bunny ears? Honestly, Taylor, if you aren't drawing him, you don't do anything at all. We do all the work, don't we?"

Scotty placed his hand on Kyle's shoulder and got an immediate yes, to which Barry mimicked a moment later.

"Hey, I can do other stuff to annoy Wesley besides artwork."

"Yeah, like what?" Kyle asked.

Frantic for an answer, Taylor scanned his mind but found it as blank as an unused sketch book. He looked to Scotty for help but only an inpatient gaze was returned. Kyle wore a sly grin, suspecting that Taylor had nothing and waited for just the right moment to rub his artsy fartsy face in it. Barry must have found something interesting on the floor as his attention was now full engrossed with it. Taylor begged his brain to come up with something and then, finally, an epiphany.

"I got it," Taylor said. "I'll be right back."

He rose from the table and started for the vending machine near the lunch line. The other three were curious about what he had in store for Wesley, but they wouldn't have to wait long.

CHAPTER 19

A Dorito Lunch Denied

L unch was a pointless period for Wesley as rarely did he even have a lunch or the money to buy one. Every once in a while, he might have a measly sandwich or perhaps have scrounged up enough change for a bag of chips, but usually he simply feasted on water from the fountain.

Generally, he sat alone on a bench outside the lunch room. Dubbed the "stink" bench, it was rare that anyone else sat there. Sometimes he'd pretend to read a text book, but he wasn't fooling anyone. They knew why he sat alone. The other students with their lunches sat in the cafeteria chatting, joking, and relaxing, but he was content just being left alone. Scotty, Taylor, and the others were in there too, and it was unlikely they'd even let him sit at a table by himself. Sometimes they came out to taunt him and other times they didn't.

Since it was impossible to predict if or when they'd come out, Wesley made it a point to leave his bench before the bell and start down the hall to his next class on the other side of the school. If he could avoid the idiot hall monitor, he usually arrived around the time the bell rung. Why, on that day, they emerged from the lunch room fifteen minutes early was a mystery to Wesley, but with the group approaching the bench, he attempted to leave only to have Barry and Scotty grab his shoulders and pull him back down. Scotty and Kyle then flanked him on either side of the bench while Taylor stood before him in front.

"Hey, Wesley," Taylor cooed. "I was feeling kind of bad about the marker thing before and I know you don't have a lunch, so I bought you some Doritos from the machine." Taylor waved the bag in front of Wesley's face. Wesley had to swallow hard to keep from slobbering all over, God was he hungry.

"Come on, Wesley, I'm giving this to you. You can have it," The hypnotic fashion with which Taylor waved the bag, combined with Wesley's hunger began weakening his common sense. It had to be a trick, but what if just for once it wasn't? What if just this one time Taylor meant it? Just this once.

"Here, I'll open it for you."

Upon Taylor unsealing the bag, Wesley was overcome with the intoxicating aroma of nacho cheese Doritos. A barely audible rumble from his stomach demanded the bag. No longer looking at Taylor's anticipating face, Wesley reached for it.

In an instant the bag flipped, the open end turned downward, and gravity snatched the Doritos from Wesley's grasp. The bright orange triangles slipped through Wesley's fingers to the floor, only to be stomped on by Taylor. Scotty joined in the stomping as Barry and Kyle shoved Wesley from the bench into the Dorito pile on the floor.

"I promised you the Doritos but I never said you could have them in the bag," Taylor said. "Take them, there're all yours."

Wesley received a few kicks from Barry and Kyle as the bell rang. Once more they evaporated down the hall, leaving Wesley, rumbling stomach and all, on the floor. He sat in the forbidden food as other students passed him by, some laughing, some gawking, some ignoring, but soon he was alone again, just him and the crumbles.

He wiped the tears from his eyes and cursed his stupidity. Oh, how hungry he was. He was about to get up when a single orange triangle caught his eye. It was a large, perfectly shaped, undamaged Dorito. Somehow this lone Dorito had escaped their feet. Wesley stared at it. It was in perfect condition but still on the floor. There was nobody around. He could gobble it up and no one would be the wiser, but he'd know. If they ever found out that he ate a floor Dorito, he'd never live it down, but there it was sitting in pristine condition mocking his hunger. No question, it was Taylor's Dorito.

Still, it was food, and he hadn't eaten since breakfast, and then it was only a bit of left over pasta, a quarter of a can of spam, and, to Wesley's shame, a small bit of cat food. He reached for the whole Dorito, put it in his mouth, and then swallowed his pride.

Envying the dead, he rose to his feet. He had another class but who cared? Scotty and Taylor were in it anyway. The front doors of the school were right down the hall. Instead of class, he could go down to the field near his house. There were apple and oak trees down there, and he could help himself to some apples and acorns. More than once these life-giving trees had kept him from going hungry. They were also peaceful and gave him not only food, but shade to retreat into from the world. Failing to find a reason to remain in school any longer, Wesley walked out.

CHAPTER 20

The Right and Left Sides of Scotty

That was so funny, Taylor," Barry said as they walked down the hall.

"Hell yeah it was," agreed Scotty, placing his arm around Taylor. "I was wrong. You know how to get someone good."

Scotty walked in the middle with Taylor and Barry to either side. Kyle meandered behind them as they strolled along. He wondered where Taylor had come up with an idea like that and envied his ability to come up with such a gem. In spite of the chiding in the lunch room, Scotty always liked Taylor's artwork and had given him many complements on it. Kyle couldn't draw to save his life and it looked as though Scotty was finding a new best friend in the artist.

When the hallway split, Taylor, Scotty, and Barry turned right, toward their next class. Kyle's next class was to the left, but when he yelped goodbye, Scotty simply waved his arm without so much as turning around. Kyle had hoped that the lunch room teasing of Taylor would continue. He enjoyed having a laugh at the artist's expense. With Taylor's Dorito bag idea though, Scotty had left him by the wayside. Later, Kyle would have to think of a way to wedge himself back in with Scotty and nudge Taylor out.

He was Scotty's best friend and that was the way it was going to stay. He was not about to be replaced by some artist who, by chance, came up with a great idea to use against that stink face. Eventually, he'd be able to show Scotty that Taylor wasn't worth having around. Sooner or later, he'd see that Taylor was just some jerk who happened to be good with crayons. At lunch, Kyle had been hopeful that Scotty saw that, but Taylor had won his way back in with that Doritos stunt. Oh well, Kyle thought, Scotty would figure it out at some point. Until then, Taylor would be a pest Kyle would have to deal with, but at the very least, he had Wesley to take his frustrations out on.

CHAPTER 21

Hello Gorgeous

Nikki stood fully nude in the bright pink room, staring at the gorgeous reflection in the full length mirror. With perfectly manicured fingernails, Nikki caressed the wonderful head of hair God saw fit to bestow. The dyed black hair Nikki loved so much was worn in a classic, straight, medium-length bob style being parted on one side and brushed over. The tips of the hair were flicked outward and left Nikki's locks simply gorgeous.

Nikki's reflection was reciprocated, smiling with pouty Raspberry Sorbet lip gloss by Maybelline and, of course, light mineral powder for that natural glow. Nikki's intense blue eyes were made even more so by the ebony black eyeliner carefully put in place. Nikki had always felt lucky to have this face. It was angular, feminine, and just plain girly.

Nikki's torso was thin but hardly famished, with little fat and well-defined, smooth muscles, made smoother by the skin creams and body washes. Nikki could never help but rub down that silky smooth, hairless skin, sometimes using only the tips of his fingers to caress his body. Because he had shaved off all his pubic hair, his penis appeared to loom large. Nikki giggled at his penis. He liked it. It was about average size and width, but without a pubic hair forest to hide in, it truly was a sight to behold. Any girl or guy would be lucky to experience it.

He twisted and turned in the mirror trying to achieve a perfect view of his freshly waxed legs. Nikki then rose to his tippy toes and twirled around to get a good look at that tight ass he adored so. It was perky and firm, made for slapping, and he gave himself one playful tap before giggling some more.

Still naked, Nikki plopped down on his pink comforter covered bed and grinned. At eighteen, Nicolas Caldwell had little joy beyond being alone in front of the mirror. Being a freakish outcast at school meant he had nothing else to do every night except come home and spend time with himself. At one point, he would come home in tears but they had dried up and now only a tear-less stone remained. Nikki couldn't remember the last time he had cried. That ability was lost long ago, leaving nothing but rage in its place.

His walls were adorned with posters of teen idols such as Justin Bieber, Zach Efron, Selena Gomez, and Vanessa Hudgens. Their gorgeous faces comforted him every night, never judging and always welcoming him into their club. In another time and place, Nikki too could have shown off his dramatic talent, but even the drama club at school scoffed at him and he was run off the stage. These were bad thoughts for Nikki to be thinking. His rage usually turned his body pinkish and then he'd begin sweating and ruin his makeup.

Nikki inhaled deeply, pushing away all the bad thoughts, then rose from the bed and opened his closet. He shifted past the mess of clothes, making his way to his prized possession kept in the back, safely out of view from his mother's nosey eyes. At last after a moment of burrowing, he found it, his sweetheart knee-length tulle lace homecoming dress.

Almost in love, he held it up, grateful to have saved it. It had belonged to his twin sister Shannon who wore it to some sweet sixteen two years back. Afterward, she had placed it in the goodwill bag, where Nikki had fished it out and nurtured it ever since. When he donned it, there was no creature on earth more beautiful. Being of a similar body type as his sister the dress fit him almost as well as it did her. Though physically similar to his sister, she too held him in disdain. When he was taunted at school she'd look in the other direction, embarrassed to share the same gene pool. When he wore makeup or girly clothes, she warned him to stay out of her closet, though he hadn't been in her closet since he was fourteen. No, Shannon was as bad as any of them. She currently was doing a semester abroad in Paris and Nikki did not miss her.

Now wearing the dress, Nikki returned to the mirror and gave a model pose and smile. Now he was truly gorgeous. Though mostly white with an all-white skirt, the dress sported a complementing black flowered bodice. The fit of the strapless ball gown was just about perfect. The knee-length hemline showed off his lower legs while enticing any wandering hand to sneak up. *Oh what a tease I am,* thought Nikki. The dress boasted embellishments of beading and lace and with just a bit of stuffing added to the built in bra, Nikki's chest commanded attention.

He reluctantly had to admit that Shannon had looked stunning in the dress, but now so did he. He pranced in front of the mirror, giving various poses and faces, thinking how lucky girls were to have so many wonderful adornments for their bodies. Things like dresses, skirts, hair spray, lip gloss, shoes, lip stick, eye liner, blush, nail polish, purses, fragrances, moisturizers, hair coloring, curling irons, eye shadow, luminizer, mineral powder, primer, cleaners, foundations of all types, mascara, false eyelashes, lip stains, lip plumpers, body makeup, and bronzers.

So many things girls took for granted that boys were denied the freedom to use. It was unfair but at least in his room, Nikki could be the beautiful boy he felt like. He began twirling, watching the dress flow as he whipped around. He was gorgeous, no matter what anyone said. The faster he spun, the more beautiful he felt and the hem encircling him flowed in agreement. He was a gorgeous boy and ecstasy followed.

CHAPTER 22

Not So Gorgeous at School

School sucked. That was a fact that anyone in Nikki's heeled leather boots couldn't deny. It was impossible to wear the dress to school, but he could still feel pretty in his low cut skin tight jeans and pink satin cling shirt. Girls were lucky, Nikki thought. They could be feminine in pants or dresses, and wearing either was no longer an issue. He watched the girls walk and copied them just about perfectly, swinging his hips and swaying his money maker. Along with his beauty, Nikki also prided himself on his sense of observation and ability to imitate.

Sooner or later, the comments would start and the evil boys would find him, but so what? He'd walk right through them and ignore the abuse as he always did. Nikki Caldwell would not run or hide. Taking abuse was what he did best, and every day Nikki simply grew colder. *My day is fast approaching*, he thought, *and when it arrives, it will be very easy to do what must be done without hesitation or regret.* He had no future and soon the school would learn that hell hath no fury like Nikki scorned.

To his surprise, he successfully finished at his locker without any harassment. Usually, he was met by insults and, when the evil boys showed up, various kinds of assaults. The stares and disdainful looks Nikki no longer cared about, but he was forever forced to watch his rear end.

Before Nikki turned in the direction of his first meaningless class, he gazed longingly at his school crushes a little way down the hall. Joel and Ashleigh were one of the more popular couples at his Parkins, Ohio, high school. He did track, she did soccer, and both were gorgeous and talented athletes with bodies to die for. Suddenly, Joel treated Nikki to a bit of eye candy when he bent over to retrieve a dropped a notebook. His rear might have been hidden by denim but Nikki grinned at his good fortune. As Joel stood upright again, he placed his arm around Ashleigh, just barely running his hand over her butt. What a great show for Nikki's lusty eyes.

It had been over a year since they had gotten together and, from a distance, Nikki admired them both. They never were mean to him, nor did they look down on him. They were some of the nice ones who simply ignored him and allowed him to exist in peace. Nikki was always grateful for that. Oh, how he wanted them, down at his feet, though. They would protest at first, but in time they would grow to love him and thank him for their domination. He would be so gentle with them, firm but gentle, and together they would all be happy.

His crushes turned and walked down the hall, and Nikki did the same. Watching them was one of the very few pleasures he had in school, but soon he'd rob this hellhole of all pleasure. The evil boys and everyone else would pay dearly for stealing his joy, his happiness, his tears. At that moment, Nikki felt a hard prod to his rear end as something invaded the sensitive space between his butt cheeks. He jumped and quickly swatted away the offending implement and scowled at having been taken by surprise by the evil boys again.

"What's the matter, Nikki?" asked Albert, a pock-faced, chunky kid with a bad attitude. "Don't faggots like things up their butts?"

He laughed and was joined by Ethan and Nate. One of their evil little games was to poke him in the rear end with anything they could find. In this case it was an umbrella, but they had also used pens, sticks, and even sometimes their own fingers.

Nikki rolled his eyes and began storming off, but the evil boys weren't about to allow him to get off so easy.

"Where're you going, faggot?" Ethan snarled as he shoved Nikki into the wall.

Nikki pushed Ethan away and tried to keep moving, but Ethan sprang back and shoved him into the wall a second time, this time harder, hurting Nikki's shoulder.

"What's the matter, faggot? You gonna cry?" Albert asked.

Nikki was not about to cry. He couldn't any longer but he also couldn't fight off these three either. He kept moving only to get another, harder poke in his rear end from the umbrella. This time the jab was so piercing that it caused Nikki to let out a girlish yelp, which gave the evil boys something else to laugh about.

"I think he's a girl." Albert laughed. "I think he's a girl!"

"Let's see," Nate said and he grabbed Nikki's groin.

Nikki shoved Nate's hands away but he continued the groping, over and over. When he couldn't get a firm grip on Nikki's manhood, Nate simply punched him in the balls. Nikki crumpled to his knees and held his privates. It was a hard shot and the three evil boys reveled in it.

"Well," Albert started. "I guess it does hurt a girl when you punch her in the pussy."

"I wonder if it'll hurt being smacked in the titties," Ethan said.

Nikki wrapped himself tightly in his arms but Ethan mercilessly began smacking his chest and doing his best to pinch his sensitive nipples. Soon Nate joined in the effort as Albert stood by laughing. In a final effort to escape, Nikki lunged forward, nearly knocking the two pinchers over and scooted away, the sounds of hateful laughter echoing in his ears. He had escaped for now, but his beautiful body had been soiled again. They would pay, and soon.

He ran into the bathroom, not noticing it was the girls' room and lifted up his shirt. His nipples and the surrounding skin were already reddening and within a few hours there would be bruises. The angry face in the mirror enraged Nikki all the more. That was not gorgeous. That was ugly and hateful. Once again, those evil boys had stolen away some of his beauty.

Beauty was a fickle thing. Once taken or lost, it was difficult to regain. Nikki was lucky to have a perfect body as well as wonderful hair and a gorgeous dress, but inner beauty could be destroyed so much easier and, worst of all, it was almost impossible to reclaim. How much beauty had those evil boys taken from him? Nikki didn't know but, at one point, he had laughed and smiled with the best of them. At one point, he was a bubbly little boy who loved everyone he met. At one point, he was happy. He remembered that, but it was a faded and broken memory, the type an Alzheimer's patient would have, a vague reminder of a life once lived but now almost finished.

"Nicolas, you were told about coming into the girls' bathroom."

He looked to the side and saw a plump, frizzy haired teacher with thick glasses out of the 1970s bearing down on him.

"I don't care what you think you are, Nicolas. This is the girl's room and you aren't one. You use the boys' room, okay."

Nikki nodded and rolled his eyes as he exited the girls' room. He might as well humor that monstrosity of a teacher. Nikki had seen her many times before. Her jelly roles around her belly jiggled when she walked, and her ridiculous hair couldn't look worse even if she stuck her tits into an electrical outlet. Nikki secretly called her the frizzy-haired planet, and he was always careful not to get too close, less he'd be sucked in by her gravity. Nikki's private little jokes at the teacher's expense made him smile a bit, but the evil boys would be around later, that was for sure.

CHAPTER 23

More of the Same for Nikki

L ater that day, Nikki stood at his locker, exchanging one heavy text book for another, when one slipped out of his hand and hit the floor. Had Nikki looked behind him he never would have bent over, but he had other things on his mind and didn't bother looking. Just as he bent over to retrieve the book, he felt a sharp, hard jab to his butt crack.

The shock of it caused him to lunge forward and cram his head into his locker. The narrow locker held his head firm as fright set in. Nikki yanked and twisted about, trying to free his head, but the space was just a little too narrow and his head too big. The evil boys swarmed from behind and prodded his rear end without mercy.

One of them, Nikki wasn't sure who, actually stuck his hand down the back of his pants and pinched his sensitive skin. Nikki growled. He cursed and thrashed about, kicking backward but never getting close to landing a shot. After more than a minute of torment, he finally yanked his head free and dropped to the floor.

The evil boys were flushed red from the hilarity, and many other students passing by joined in the gawking. When he rose from the ground to escape, Nate made one last grab at his crotch. Finally, however, Nikki was able to evade the hand, shove Nate into the wall, and bolt down the hall. Nate might remember that later, but for the moment Nikki escaped.

He ducked into a stairwell and listened to his heart jackhammer his chest wall. His head ached a bit but he wasn't scratched by the locker. His rear end hurt much more from the abuse it had taken and, with the fright in the past, the seething began. His ass was not a pin cushion, but it was to them, something to amuse their sick, twisted desires with. These ugly, evil boys couldn't stand the sight of something so beautiful, so naturally they had to destroy it.

For a moment, Nikki thought he would burst and finally break down in tears, but they couldn't come. He tried to force them out. He whined, he moaned, he scrunched his eyes and heaved his chest, but nothing. That emotional release was gone and could not be resurrected. What other method of release did he have? Nothing! He would have to carry it inside.

"Nicolas, what are you doing here? The stairwell is not a place to stand around."

Nikki looked over to the fat, frizzy-haired pest he seemed unable to rid himself of. It was as if she waited until just after his torments to kick him when he was at his weakest. That was it, she knew what was going on and quietly approved. She would watch from the distance as her gorgeous rival was brought down a notch and then would move in to finish off the slaughter. She was like a vulture, eagerly awaiting the pride of lions to vacate the kill before snuffing up whatever was left.

"Do you have any idea what just happened to me?" Nikki asked.

"Watch your tone, Nicolas," she warned, raising a single pudgy finger.

"My name is Nikki," he said firmly.

"I've seen your records. It says Nicolas on them and that is what I'll call you. Now, not another word. Report to your next class."

Nikki stormed passed her, this time making sure she noticed his look of disdain. She returned the gaze, obviously jealous that a boy could be so much more beautiful than her. Good lord, Nikki thought, did she exist on a diet of Big Macs and soda? Was the word "salad" even in her vocabulary? What about exercise? For Christmas, maybe he'd buy her a dictionary so she could look these things up herself. While he was at it, maybe he'd also pick up a meat cleaver and put that to good use as well, perhaps feed a few homeless families with her trimmings. Nikki grinned, admiring his generous spirit.

Another aspect Nikki loved about himself was his ability to carry on in spite of the pain and humiliation. Sooner or later they'd all pay but, in the meantime, he would not curl up and die and those evil boys knew it. They could beat him, they could belittle him, they could pinch, punch, and slap him about. They could crush him beneath their sludge coated Nikes, but they couldn't destroy him. Perhaps, he was a pin cushion, after all, but one that could take endless pins and needles. Who knew how many pins they had jabbed into him already? But sooner or later he'd spit those pins right back at them.

CHAPTER 24

An Angry Crush

Albert, Ethan, and Nate took a seat at their usual lunch table. Nikki was at his customary corner table, but at the moment they paid him no attention. It was lunch time and their thoughts dwelled entirely on their stomachs. Albert sat on one side of the table, while Ethan and Nate sat across from him. A few other boys joined them and the eating commenced.

"Hey, Albert," stated one skinny spikey haired kid. "That was pretty funny what you did to Nikki this morning."

Albert chuckled at the comment and choked a bit on

his hoagie. "Thanks, I can't stand that stupid faggot."

"Yeah, he's nasty—or she's nasty—whatever it is, Nikki's nasty," Spikey said.

"The weird thing is that you'd think that faggot would enjoy a poke in the ass from an umbrella," Nate said. "He didn't though."

The boys laughed at Nate's keen observation and continued eating. Mostly, they chatted about school work, girls, and video games. Ethan told a long rambling story of his conquest in some recently released war game which had everyone enthralled, everyone except Albert, who sat quietly and paid no attention to his friend's impressive feat.

Albert finished his bologna and cheese hoagie and wiped the remnant of creamy mayo from his mouth. He opened his bag of chips and savored the thought of a cupcake waiting for him in his lunch bag, along with a cold machine bought Mountain Dew to wash it all down. Lunch was about eating, not talking, and Albert only rarely put a word in with his friends. Mostly, Ethan and Nate led the conversation while Albert tended to the matter of filling his belly.

While his friends chatted of video game warfare, Albert ate and stole glances across the room at the object of his rage, Nikki. He was careful of how he looked at Nikki, never directly, only through casual glances out the corner of his eye. God, how he hated that faggot. Albert was far more observant than his friends and was able to make out the finer points of Nikki's disgusting behavior. Ethan and Nate could see Nikki's skin tight clothes, but Albert could make out the seductive swing of his hips when he walked. Ethan and Nate could see Nikki's makeup, but Albert noticed the pin point precision with which Nikki applied his lip gloss. Ethan and Nate could see his long girlish hair, but Albert saw how it bounced and flowed, complimenting Nikki's every move.

Albert silently cursed Nikki as he stuffed a handful full of chips down his throat. Why did Nikki have to be like that? Nobody should be like that. Faggots were disgusting. Albert observed as Nikki, unaware he was being watched, ran his hands over his chest, smoothing his blouse. From there he whipped out some kind of cream and lathered it over his hands. Albert saw Nikki grin after looking at his hands, satisfied with their silky smoothness.

The other boys at his table faded away as Albert's attention fell solely on Nikki, his bouncy hair, his smooth skin, his feminine face, his tight clothes. Girls were supposed to be pretty, not boys. And then the rage set in. No, Nikki was not pretty! Albert did not just think that. Nikki was a freak, a freak that was making him think bad thoughts, the kinds of thought you made about girls. Nikki wasn't a girl. He was a faggot!

After rinsing his hatred down with a swig of Mountain Dew, Albert peered down to his crotch and to his horror, recognized the silhouette of a full blown erection. That rotten faggot! He had done it again. Oh, he would pay for this. Oh yes, Nikki would pay for giving him an erection, but first, before getting up and before any of his friends noticed, Albert had to rid of himself of the faggot-infected erection.

He leaned forward into the table and placed his left hand underneath. He curled his hand into a fist and silently struck the erection. Pain exploded in all directions as his penis recoiled. His forehead broke out with sweat and his face went scarlet. Albert gritted his teeth to keep from crying out and tensed every muscle in his body in a futile effort to dull the pain.

A few moments later, the pain became more manageable but Albert still had to wipe a rogue tear from his eye. He hated having to strike himself, but it was the only way to be rid of the sickness that Nikki infected him with. It didn't happen often, just when he looked at Nikki for too long. Every once in a while, he'd wind up with a major boner because of Nikki, and it was only a matter of time before the others found out. The only treatment for Nikki's spells was beating him and making his life miserable. If Albert was constantly tortured, then Nikki would be too. If only Nikki would change, Albert decided, then this problem would be solved.

Albert looked down at his belly and then felt his

pock-scarred face. Not only did Nikki force faggot thoughts into his head, but he also flaunted his beauty for all to see.

Albert couldn't deny it. Nikki was beautiful—gorgeous—and had to be destroyed. Albert shook his head quickly, afraid of getting another erection. Thoughts of Nikki brought them on quick.

"Hey, Albert, you okay?" Ethan's sudden question brought Albert back to the table.

"I'm fine," Albert said. "Why?"

"Well, your face is all red," Ethan said.

"It's hot," Albert said. "It's very hot in here."

"It doesn't feel that hot in here," said a boy sitting next to Ethan

"Well, it is. It's too hot in here," Albert said.

"Look at that," Nate started, forgetting all about Albert's heat problem. "Nikki's putting on lipstick."

All the boys, including Albert, peered over and saw that Nikki was indeed reapplying. Albert recognized that it was lip gloss and not lipstick but didn't mention it.

"What is wrong with that faggot?" Nate asked.

"A lot," Albert stated. He took another sip from his Mountain Dew and looked across the table at Ethan and Nate.

"A lot is wrong with Nikki," Albert said "And as soon as I'm done with my soda, we're going to go over and find out what."

Ethan and Nate smiled as encouragement flowed from the other boys. Albert's mountain Dew was more than half empty and he took another big gulp.

CHAPTER 25

Lunch Room Warfare

Nikki claimed a table in the corner as his own. No one would sit with him, but at least he was never challenged for his spot. The cafeteria aids' routine was as reliable as the evil boys'.

They would hang around in the cafeteria, watching the students for about fifteen minutes, and then they would step out to chat in private and have a smoke. Technically, it was against school rules, but what were rules compared the smooth pleasure of nicotine and rat poison rolled into a stick? Still, their fifteen minutes in the lunch room did give Nikki enough time to eat before the evil boys came over. They wouldn't start before the aids left, but once they did, it wouldn't be long before the lunch time abuse began.

Nikki watched the useless aids carefully as they pulled their cigarettes out of their overstuffed purses. They laughed and chatted as they walked to the side door for a cancer stick, not noticing the eyes of the students on them. They knew the routine too. As soon as the aids left, they were in for a real show, staring Nikki and the evil boys. Albert's head perked up and shook like a dog eager to go out. From across the room, he threw Nikki a sadistic smile with his lips curled all the way up to his ears and his brow furrowed. It was almost Showtime.

Nikki quickly packed up his backpack, intent on leaving the lunch room. Sometimes he could escape down the hall and hide in a bathroom until lunch was over, other times he was caught, sometimes by the frizzy-haired planetoid, and forced to return. It could go either way, but he always had to try. The reality was that the evil boys had nearly thirty minutes reserved for torturing him, and nobody ever stepped in. God forbid, the aids put out their cigarettes and did their jobs watching the students.

Nikki slipped out of the cafeteria and trotted down the hall, watching behind him. The evil boys rarely followed, but if he stayed in the cafeteria, they would jump on him. If he left, then they got their kicks for having forced him out, but at least he escaped from them. He was halfway to a safe bathroom when he heard his name called from behind. Without having to turn around, he knew it was none other than the frizzy haired planet. She probably stalked out in the hall just waiting to trap him.

"You really are being difficult today, aren't you?" she asked, sporting a proud smirk. "I'm glad I came this way. You're always sneaking around."

"I left the lunch room to get away from guys who want to hurt me," Nikki said bluntly.

"Honestly, Nikki, you aren't hurt and you never have been. I see you every day. You're a drama queen and we both know it, and let's face facts, is it really such a surprise you aren't accepted?"

She ended her sentence with a grin, having tasted victory. Nikki sensed she'd celebrate later with a victory soda and perhaps a chili dog with fries on the side. Unsure of why he was even obeying her, he returned to the lunch room, preferring the evil boys' abuse over hers. He settled back into his chair and waited for them to notice his return. At first, they were far too busy acting like a group of jackasses toward several giggling idiot girls to notice him. They were just too funny with their un-witty jokes and loud noises. Honestly, Nikki mused, was this a school or a barn yard? After a few moments of sitting, someone did point Nikki out to Albert and then the real show began.

When they started over, Nikki got up and tried to keep the table in between him and them, but that plan was easily overcome by Albert and Ethan starting around one way, and Nate the other. Ethan reached him first and gave his hair a tug. Nikki recoiled and stumbled into Nate, who smeared something greasy into his hair.

"Ha, ha, with your dirty black hair and that mayo I just put in it, you look like a skunk," Nikki pushed passed Nate, wiping the mayo off as the three enjoyed a cheap laugh.

"You cretins are disgusting," Nikki exclaimed, wiping his hair.

"Look at you, fag, with your makeup and clothes, you're disgusting."

After Albert's excuse for a comeback, he connected his meaty open palm to Nikki's face and dropped him to his knees. Nikki looked up just in time to receive another open palm to the top of his head.

Although dazed by the blows, Nikki had enough sense to dive under the table, the last sanctuary available, but Ethan grabbed his leg and tried tugging him back out. Nikki pulled away and attempted to rise to his feet but he stumbled into Nate for the second time and crashed to the floor. With Nikki now on top, Nate wrapped him into a one armed headlock head lock and began spanking his rear end with all the force he could muster.

"Stop being a fag! Stop being a fag!" Over and over

he struck Nikki's bottom, striking hardest when screaming "fag."

Nikki kicked and squealed but Nate was far too
strong and all he could do was struggle in vain.

Albert and Ethan nearly died of laughter, as well as
much of the live cafeteria audience. Finally, after more
than twenty smacks, Nikki squirmed away again and took
refuge under the table. To get him out meant flipping the
table and Nikki doubted they'd do that, if only because
they wouldn't think of it.

"Come on, Nikki," Albert yelled. "Come back out
and play." He chucked Nikki's backpack at him clocking
him in the face. "Hell yeah, got him."

Nate giggled. "Great shot."

While Albert and Nate celebrated whacking Nikki
with his own backpack, Ethan had found a broom from
somewhere and began poking at him under the table.

"When my cat hides under the bed, this is how I get
him out."

Using the pole end of the broom, Ethan poked and
prodded Nikki up and down, trying to coax him out from
under the table.

"Leave me alone!" Nikki screamed, but the evil boys
just hooted and hollered and Ethan poked harder. Unable
to escape the broom handle and unwilling to leave his
refuge, Nikki grabbed the broom and yanked.

Nikki's desperation tug on the broom pulled Ethan

forward causing him to crack his head against the edge of the table. With his head throbbing, Ethan dropped the broom and stumbled away, cursing and shouting. Albert and Nate forgot about Nikki for the moment and rushed to aid Ethan who, while not bleeding, was moaning and cradling his head.

Nikki pulled the broom firmly into his clutches, ready to use his new found weapon if they dared come back, but at that moment the smoking aids returned from their nicotine-filled gossiping session and started for Ethan. Nikki wondered what they would tell them. He doubted they would admit the truth to the aids. Nikki could just imagine Ethan telling the aids that the faggot currently cowering under the table beat him up. Highly unlikely, Nikki thought. While he did not hear every word said, Nate definitely mentioned something about Ethan tripping over a bag and smacking his head on the floor. With Nate and the aids' help, they rushed Ethan to the nurse. Albert waited behind until they were gone then knelt back down by Nikki's table.

Nikki clutched the broom ready for a one on one, but Albert just glared.

"You're going to pay for that one. Just wait."

Before Nikki could respond, Albert shot up and jogged after his friends and the aids. In another few minutes the bell would ring, so Nikki remained huddled under the table with his broom, trying to keep from trembling with fright. Those evil boys. Those evil, rotten boys! They deserved to be chopped up in to little pieces. They deserved to be castrated with rusted fishhooks. Death was too kind for the likes of them!

Nikki clutched the broom till his knuckles turned white. He held his trophy for all it was worth but, for the first time, in spite of the pain and humiliation, he had gotten the better of them. The stupid little broom was proof. No matter what lay over the horizon as a result of the fight, they couldn't take this away from him. Let Albert make his threats. Look at the big bad evil boy now. With his buddies he was tough as nails but wouldn't come after him under the table when alone. Maybe he would regret it later but for the first time, Nikki could claim a sliver of victory. When the bell rang, he rushed to his locker and placed the broom in it. He had earned it and the broom just fit. Nikki then grabbed his afternoon books and strutted down the hall.

CHAPTER 26

An Ambulance Ride Down Memory Lane

Perhaps Ethan had a concussion. It was suspected but not yet known. They'd run some tests at the hospital to find out. Though his head hurt, his pride throbbed. That miserable faggot somehow got a lucky shot and now he lay in a speeding ambulance. The two EMTs in the back with him told him to lay still and Ethan was following directions. They assured him that these types of injuries happened all the time.

"Accidents will happen," one of them said.

Ethan lay on the stretcher, jostling slightly back and forth as they weaved through traffic, playing the movie in his head over and over. It was pretty short, more of a clip rather than a whole movie. The faggot had simply grabbed the broom and pulled him into a table. It was so stupid, how could Nikki have won that. One of these days, he'd kill that faggot, all faggots. They all deserved to die.

Ethan had not even known what a faggot was until he was ten. At that age he and his Uncle Lonnie had had sex a few times. Sometimes orally, other times anally. It went on for a little while until Uncle Lonnie got killed in a hunting accident. A buddy of Lonnie's had inadvertently shot him in the back. Ethan knew the man's son and saw them both after the accident. They both seemed to handle their grief with quiet grace. It was explained to him that they were just in shock from the whole ordeal. Ethan had accepted that.

Ethan never told anyone about the encounters, but after Uncle Lonnie's death, he knew enough to declare war on faggots. The faggot creatures who had sex with little boys and called it love. Uncle Lonnie was a faggot. He told Ethan he loved him and that their love was natural but misunderstood. He always told Ethan that one day this type of love would be accepted but until then they had to keep it secret.

"You love Uncle Lonnie, don't you?" he'd say. "Then you need to protect me and not talk about our love."

Ethan told him that he loved him and, in return, was given presents. Uncle Lonnie got him a new bike, an XBOX, and took him to baseball games. Uncle Lonnie could be nice, but at the end of the day he was still a faggot.

Well, Nikki wouldn't love any little boys. With Nate and Albert's help, Nikki would be destroyed and there would be one less faggot in the world. Sooner or later Ethan would be rid of Nikki and all that had been done to him would cease to matter. Sooner or later, he'd have his justice over Nikki and all other faggots.

CHAPTER 27

Bathroom Prey

The remainder of the day was almost good, or at least as good as was possible for Nikki. While in the hall heading toward his last class, he strolled by the frizzy-haired planet and gave her a cheerful grin, which was answered with a scowl. So this was happiness, like an eternal piece of chocolate fudge in his mouth, oh how sweet. Finally, after having been robbed so many times by the evil boys, he'd snatched a morsel from them. Hooray for Nikki!

Had he known what cloud nine was, he surely would have agreed that he was soaring on it. The problem with flying high, however, was that it was a long way down, and the higher you went, the greater the drop. At the end of the day, Nikki made a stop in the boy's room and took a seat in a stall. He placed a layer of toilet paper over the porcelain god like any normal person would do. He then took his seat, hoping his business would not take too long. He had some time but didn't want to miss the bus.

After dropping what he considered to be a cute little turd into the bowl, he began hearing voices. Not so much voices but whispers, very low whispers. Having spent most of his life as a prey animal, Nikki had developed keen instincts and knew when trouble was afoot. The lone turd in the bowl had friends patiently waiting to greet the world, but they would have to wait for the toilet at home. He needed to escape now.

Silently, he rose to his feet and pulled up his tight jeans. Flushing the toilet might arouse the suspicions of the ones he was sure were in the bathroom with him, so his turd would remain un-flushed. They sensed he was in the bathroom. Nikki was sure of that, but they hadn't figured out which stall yet. Escape was impossible, but perhaps he could hide from them. It was his only chance.

He softly stepped up onto the toilet seat, hoping that if they peered under the stall, they wouldn't notice any feet. He looked down into the brown filled toilet bowl and prayed his boots wouldn't slip. He silently sighed. His crap stunk like everyone else's.

Another whisper perked his ears once again, like a rabbit on high alert. Nikki thought he caught the phrase "not in here" followed by "I know he is." He couldn't quite discern who said what, but the predators were lurking and they wouldn't give up until satisfied. Nikki swallowed hard and prayed they couldn't hear him breathing or detect his heart pounding in fright. *Please*, he begged silently, *don't let them smell my fear.* But predators always could.

Sweat now coated his face and Nikki peered down in horror. His backpack still sat on the ground just inside the stall door. Even if they couldn't see his feet up on the toilet, they would certainly see the pink and purple backpack and then move in for the kill. He was in the last stall and the whispers hadn't reached him, perhaps there was yet time to lose their scent.

Nikki bent his knees and began lowering himself to reach for the backpack. He squatted down with the murky water threatening from below, the ugly brown begging him to slip and give himself away. He bent over, his hand now a few inches from grasping the backpack, when a chunky shadow emerged from in front of the stall door. Nikki froze in his bent over squatting stance, as the chunky shadow swayed from side to side, as if debating how to pounce.

The strain of Nikki's squat increased his sweating. A bead formed on his forehead and from its birthplace migrated down between his eyes. It continued its journey south on the right side of his nose past his mouth, narrowly avoiding his gaping tongue.

The bead ran out of road at Nikki's jawline and fell to the floor.

The predator, as if smelling the fallen bead, moved suddenly and the stall door flung open.

The exploding door jostled Nikki and he slipped from the toilet seat, sinking his right boot into the water. Nikki screamed and stumbled to the side as Albert rushed in. The prey curled up into a ball, unable to escape the chunky punches striking all over.

"You faggot, you faggot! Ethan probably has a concussion because of you," Albert yelled.

"He deserved it," Nikki bellowed, and the punching continued.

Most of the punches hit him in the back and arms, but a few got through to his head and face and Nikki's nose bled. The stall was too narrow for Nate to fit in and join the beating so he settled for shouting encouragement from outside.

"You think this is funny? You think this is funny?" Albert seized Nikki's hair and rammed his head into the side of the stall.

Nikki grabbed Albert's hands and dug his nails deeply into his flesh. This hurt the beast and made him bleed but did nothing to stop him.

Albert, using all his bulk, yanked Nikki up by the hair and kneed him in the stomach. At once Nikki couldn't breathe. All the air was stolen and only gasps remained.

Another open-palmed smack to the head sent Nikki's battered body against the toilet, and he looked down at the water beginning to absorb the brown. A monstrous hand snatched the back of his hair and began pushing forward. Nikki's strength was nothing compared to Albert's. He tried pushing off the toilet, but Albert pressed harder, now using both hands, and Nikki's head lurched dangerously close to the water.

"You're eating it, Nikki. You're eating it," Albert cried.

"Stop it!" Nikki screamed, but the demand landed on hate-filled deaf ears.

Albert wasn't stopping but he wasn't gaining ground either. Nikki realized the chunky monster was out of breath. Albert's strength dwarfed his, but Nikki had endurance and stamina on his side. Using the toilet as leverage, he pushed up from the brown water. The tide of the fight had now turned and Albert was fast losing control over Nikki. Soon Albert's strength would be depleted and his goal of stuffing Nikki's head into the soiled toilet would be thwarted.

Nikki couldn't win a fight, but maybe he could escape a wet brown head. It would be a small victory but one Nikki craved. With his head gaining distance from the water, Nikki pulled his leg forward, stealing more leverage from Albert. Almost, Nikki thought. Albert was nearly on his knees losing the edge to his prey. Nikki felt Albert's desperation climbing as his strength depleted.

He kept pushing off the toilet, forcing Albert back. The tide was turning. Albert could grind on him all he liked, but Nikki continued putting distance between his head and the toilet, inch by inch. In a last sputtering attempt to snatch victory back from his prey, Albert began heaving his pelvis into Nikki's behind, yet still Nikki continued up. Albert's grip was loosening. What little strength and leverage he still held was vanishing like steam into the air. Only his sheer weight advantage kept control over Nikki now, and soon that too would fail. Albert gasped in horror, knowing Nikki was about to escape.

On some subconscious level both boys knew that it was a simple fact of nature that in the short term brute strength is indomitable, but without a marriage to endurance and stamina, it quickly putters out. The struggle could not last much longer. Albert was nearly out of gas, having burnt out his brute strength advantage too early. The faggot was now rising. Nikki however, had forgotten another sad but true fact of nature: strength in numbers. He remembered this lesson only after Nate joined the fray.

Nate, fresh from the sidelines, dog piled on top of Nikki and Albert. Under this fresh weight Nikki's arms collapsed and his head plunged into the brown. In disgust and horror Nikki thrashed about, water filling his nose and mouth. Twisting his head from side to side allowed some wretched air to reach his lungs, but the poisoned air was a mere one step above drowning. The evil boys laughed as the toilet roared and the water began to whirl-pool. Albert had flushed. The sucking pulled his hair far-ther into the bowl until the toilet held him in place all by itself. When Albert and Nate realized the toilet had joined their team, they began punching Nikki about the sides of his body and then kicking hard in the rear end.

"I told you you'd drink your crap Nikki," Albert yelled and he punched Nikki in the side again.

Nate continued striking from behind as Nikki fought and kicked about, hollering at the top of his lungs, but knowing that no one was coming. The assault only stopped when Nate said they would miss their bus if they continued.

Albert leaned over into the toilet and whispered, "Don't ever mess around with us again."

With that the pair fled the bathroom, leaving Nikki in the toilet. Nate giddily cackled at the feat they just ac-complished. Albert was more sullen, staying behind Nate and turning toward the wall slightly, horrified his friend might see his erection.

"We totally flushed that fag!" Nate cried.

"Yeah," Albert said, leaning against the lockers.

"Hell yeah, wait'll we tell Ethan. He'll be so mad he missed it! 'Flush' and down the toilet. And then he got stuck!"

Nate hooted and hollered down the hall as Albert begged his erection to dissipate, but it wouldn't. Just like Nikki, that rock solid dick in his pants wouldn't go away. The dick bulged, begging Nate to see it. Albert hated his traitor of a penis.

He could picture it. Nate would yell, "Hey, Albert's a faggot too."

Well, he wasn't a faggot. He had some issues, yes. Albert would admit that to himself but he wasn't any faggot. He liked girls, not boys! He wasn't any faggot!

"Albert, what's up? You okay?" Nate asked.

"Yeah—I think Nikki might have kicked me in there," he lied.

"Did he get you in the dick or something?" Nate tried peering around to get a closer look at Albert's crotch, but Albert turned his back on Nate, denying him the view.

"No. No—not in the dick, near the dick—to the side—just to the side," Albert stammered, praying Nate would accept that. "Just go to your bus, Nate. I'll be fine. I just want a minute alone here. I'll be out in a second. That faggot just got a lucky shot at me."

"All right, Albert, I'll see you tomorrow I guess. You sure you're okay?"

"I'm fine, Nate, just need a minute. Go to your bus."

Nate reluctantly trotted down the hall, leaving Albert and his nearly discovered erection alone. That had been close, too close. This erection was stubborn. It refused to go down and threatened to keep him from making the bus. Hate welled up inside him once again as he balled his fist and gave his erection the Nikki treatment. This time it was harder than at lunch and Albert doubled over to his knees. The pain infected his stomach and threatened to make him vomit. Luckily, the nausea passed quickly and he just gently rocked back and forth, trying to sooth himself.

When able, Albert rose from the floor, wiped his sweaty face, and blotted his teary eyes. Tears of pain or of hate or both? Albert wasn't sure and didn't care. One of these days he was going to kill that faggot and then his problem would be solved forever. For the moment, however, he settled for the erection abating. Once it had finally gone away, Albert stood upright, adjusted his pants, and limped out to catch his bus.

❧❧❧

The evil boys might have vanished but the toilet continued holding Nikki's hair firmly and would not let go.

Still heaving from the smell and taste of the water, Nikki pulled and slowly the toilet began relinquishing his hair. When it did, Nikki snapped back in exhaustion and collapsed on his back.

Soaking and stinking, he lay on the bathroom floor for a long time just breathing good air, thankful to no longer have to fill his lungs with toilet breath. He finally sat up, pushed his sopping, smelly hair from his face, and slowly rose to his feet. The toilet might have let him go but it kept a lock of his hair as a souvenir. His gorgeous locks were ruined. Without flushing, he closed the broken stall door and stumbled over to the sink. His makeup was smudged beyond repair, his hair a wretched mess with brown smeared in, his nose and lip bled, his cheek and jaw showed the early signs of swelling, most of his perfect fingernails were broken, his blouse was ripped, his jeans were stained, and the right boot which had plunged into the toilet's mouth was soaked through. He was so…ugly.

Without a tear, he retrieved his backpack, which had been kicked into a neighboring stall during the struggle. He needed to get home to the shower. Nikki had a long walk ahead of him, but it was a breezy day and he hoped the wind would help air out his violated body.

CHAPTER 28

Such Parental Concern Over an Online Boy

Nikki washed the abuse down the shower drain, some of it anyway. His body was horribly battered. He regretted wiping the steam from the mirror as now he could see his own wretchedness. His arms, chest, back, and face were a twisted rainbow of red, purple, black, and blue.

Nikki wrapped a jumbo pink towel around his torso, covering him from chest to thighs, and tied a second smaller towel around his hair before leaving the steamy bathroom. Once back in his room, he gently settled into his desk chair, his rear end very sore. He rubbed his face,

wiping away an imaginary tear. He then embraced himself with his arms and rocked slowly in his chair, trying
to imagine the comfort he might feel if he had someone
to hold him. Oh how he wished he could cry, to just let it
all out, just once. His attempts at tears were in vain and
his eyes remained stoic and parched. The tears weren't
coming, not now, not ever. It was just as well, Nikki decided, as two pairs of footsteps approached his room.

One thing that always bothered Nikki about his parents was their tendency to knock as they opened his door.
They never knocked, waited for an answer, and then entered. No, they knocked as they barged in. How rudely
"considerate" of them. This time was no different as the
knocks emanated from the already half open door.

"Nicolas, we need to talk," his father started.

Nikki's father, with his ridiculous comb over, stood
before him. His obedient bird-like mother perched directly behind him ready to agree with whatever he said. Nikki knew the annoyed tone of voice well. It looked like
Daddy was a bit peeved about something. Poor guy, he
probably had a trying day. Maybe he was mad about
something Nikki said or did, or how he was born. Who
knew? But Nikki was certain that his self-important father and squeaky mother were about to make a series of
excellent points. Nikki grinned a bit, loving his private
sarcasm.

"We got a call from the school today. One of your

teachers said you were very rude. That won't do, Nicolas."

Nikki rolled his eyes, seeing no point in guessing which teacher had phoned home. "Teachers don't like me, nobody does. Today was a horrible day," he said, knowing the reaction he'd get.

"Well, Nikki, you can't be rude to teachers, and as for other kids not liking you, can you figure out why? You dress like a girl, act like one, wear makeup…I mean really, I only half tolerate you myself sometimes," Nikki's father said.

"Maybe a nice haircut would help," suggested his mother. "You know something shorter and manlier."

"A haircut would make a nice start," his father agreed.

"I like my hair the way it is," Nikki said. "This is how I am."

"Well then, I have no sympathy for you," his father said. "You gotta bend with the world a little bit because it won't bend for you. You wanna be left out, continue acting this way."

"I'd love to just be left out, but they come after me. I've been beaten up before you know," Good God, did he have to draw them a picture?

"You know what, Nicolas?" his father stated. "If you were picked on so much, why hasn't that made something of a man out of you? Really, be a man and defend yourself. You haven't done that, have you? I thought so. You're acting like a drama queen."

Nikki's mother stepped forward and placed her hand on her husband's shoulder. "You're being a bit harsh, dear, but, Nicolas, if you were maybe just a little bit more like a man, it might help. That's why I suggested a nice haircut. I'll even take you shopping. We can get some nice jeans, and maybe some polo shirts. That plus the haircut, I think, would do wonders for you." Nikki's mother threw him a hopeful glance, figuring that even after years of being girly, Nikki would certainly wish to change on a dime. Her deluded hope, however, was dashed by Nikki's eyes rolling, which traced the circumference of his sockets.

"I like the way I am, Mom. It's everybody else that's the problem," Nikki sneered.

"Oh yes, that's it," his father cried. "The whole world is against you. It's you against the world. You are that important! Oh, and another thing, do you have any idea how hard we sometimes have it because of you?"

Nikki couldn't help but smile at that question. He had been waiting patiently for the self-pity to emerge. It always came back to them. How did others see poor Mr. and Mrs. Caldwell with their girly, faggy son? Really now, how could they have such a spectacular daughter and such a loser son at the same time? Something must be amiss in that household.

Nikki looked his father in the eye, eager to hear the forthcoming speech.

"Your mother has to take these kinds questions all the time from the ladies in the beauty shop. You know how those gossiping hens are."

Nikki's mother looked down and reddened a bit. Her husband had a point, though. They were her friends, but their constant questions sometimes embarrassed her.

"And me at the office, they ask why I don't have any pictures of you on my desk. I tell them you're camera shy and then I crop you out of the pictures."

Nikki nodded and gently sat down on the bed. He crossed his legs and gave his daddy a warm girly smile. His grumbling father turned away and walked to the other side of the room. Point one, Nikki, and he wondered when the other half of the lecture would come. *Come on, Dad, don't keep me waiting. Tell me about your desire to get into politics.* Nikki didn't have to wait long. As soon as his father recovered from Nikki's flirtations, he started right in.

"You know I'd like to run for the city council. I have a lot of friends in this town and I could win, but we both know you and your antics could be a problem, especially down the road. What if I someday want to run for state senate? You'd be an issue. I'm not happy about it, but problem family members always come up."

"I'm sorry I'm such a problem, Dad."

"We love you very much," his mother said, trying to pacify him. "But you can be difficult with all your girly things. Many of our friends don't even want you near their sons."

More accurately, Nikki didn't want to be near their sons. To be fair, some of them were hot as hell, but that attraction only extended to the physical. Nikki also found it amusing that they were wary of their sons being near him but didn't warn their daughters, though they were just as gorgeous in Nikki's eyes.

"You need to shape up in school. You have no idea how difficult it is tolerating you, Nicolas."

His father started for the door, intent on making a grand exit after his highly important lecture. Just before exiting, his son called him back and showed off a wide feminine smile.

"Dad?"

"What?"

"My name is Nikki."

With that Nikki's father sneered and stormed out. His mother stood by for a moment before sighing and following her husband. Nikki closed the door, proud of his victory over the two of them. Nevertheless, he had to give them credit where it was due. His parents provided food, shelter, clothing (although the clothes were not to their liking), and they didn't beat him. That is what they gave him, and that was all. Nikki was well accustomed to their tolerance and accepted it. His parents thought they had gotten a beautiful girl and boy together, but instead they got a girl and something else that was not quite one or the other. How sad for them. Nikki sighed and sat down at his computer.

CHAPTER 29

Nikki and His Boys

With a miserable day of school behind him, Nikki sat down to the one of the few things that gave him pleasure in his lonely little life, his boys. Nikki loved his boys dearly and chatted with them almost every night. He nurtured his boys in a way they had never felt and, in doing so, they consoled one another and gave each other the strength to endure another day. His boys knew nothing of each other, nor the fact that Nikki was actually a boy too, but what did it matter if everybody won in the end, after losing all day long?

He had found each of them months before, wallowing in various chat rooms, and it was better they talked to him rather than some internet pervert who targeted vulnerable boys. Getting them to trust him took time. His poor boys were so beaten down and abused that the simple ability to trust had all but been extinguished. Now he had them, though. They had each other. Perhaps their parents were inadequate, perhaps their teachers were uncaring, perhaps they spent their days hiding from demons and their nights secluded and lonely. Perhaps life was unbearable, but at least they had each other, and Nikki would take care of them.

He rarely spoke of his personal problems. He preferred to listen and, in nurturing them, he nurtured his own wounded maternal instinct. Giving them hope gave him confidence that he was a nice boy, after all, reaching out to other nice boys who had been rejected. He listened to their problems, he empathized with their lives, and he promised them justice. That was most important. Justice must be served.

The crimes these poor boys endured could not be ignored, such terrible abuse at the hands of their own personal evil boys. *My poor Gregory*, Nikki mused. A spazzy and awkward boy, who had difficulty expressing himself but deep down was a good soul. Well, he was at one point. Now he was a broken shell devoid of anything except murderous rage and possessing but one saving grace, videogames. *And me, of course*. All his boys had Nikki. Gregory would soon have justice.

My poor Ronald, Nikki continued. Another nice, sensitive boy with a bad body, a body not tolerated in high school, a fat one. Girls might attack their equals they perceive as a threat, but evil boys looked for weaker prey to feast on. Nature denied Ronald any physical strength. Nature was evil and evil boys sprang from nature. Ronald once had inner strength, but that was snatched away from him little by little until only a fat hollow shell remained. Ronald's only saving grace, besides Nikki of course, was food, lots and lots of food, but food was not justice, and Ronald would have justice.

Again Nikki's thoughts shifted, this time to Wesley. *My poor Wesley*. Being born into poverty, that wasn't his fault. These so called middle-class evil boys believed themselves to be superior to this poor boy. What Wesley lacked in material wealth he made up for in heart. At least he once had heart before his evil boys robbed him of that one precious possession. Now only a poor boy remained, a poor boy longing for justice. His family was no help and, save Nikki, all he had were his magazines and his fantasies of things he'd never have. But Wesley would have justice.

Yes, Nikki's boys were tortured creatures who deserved better than circumstances had given them, and he allowed all of them to look to him to make their lives a little better. When Gregory would tell him about his bathroom ceiling locker and head shaking treatments, Nikki would sooth him. When Ronald told him about the breast slaps and yanked underwear, Nikki would calm him. When Wesley told him about the drawings, beatings, and false promises of food, Nikki fed him love. Nikki loved his boys and took care of them.

Perhaps the time had come to give his boys their days in the sun. It would be the last days of their miserable lives but it would also be their best. Nikki prided himself for his selflessness. Forcing them to live such awful lives just so he could care for them would be selfishness at its worse, like a family keeping a brain dead loved one on life support, if only to avoid the pain of burying them.

Nikki was not that selfish. He had the responsibility to fulfill his promise and give them justice, as well as take some of his own. He had groomed and nurtured his boys well over the past several months. They loved and trusted him. They all considered him their online girlfriend, although Nikki felt more like a mother. A mother that would not keep her children tied to her to protect them. Nikki would not hold them back for his own sake. He would not deny them the chance at reaching their full potential. No, he would allow his children to fly.

Nikki's plan was quite simple. There would be a week of terror, with each one of his boys taking his justice at a time. Gregory would be first on Monday, Ronald on Tuesday, Wesley on Wednesday, and Thursday would belong to Nikki. He and his boys were sick of life. They had ceased caring long ago and now the time was ripe for justice. He and his boys were the walking dead, so actual death meant nothing. Nikki had his boys trained well. If taken alive they would never talk. Let the cops try to pry information out. He doubted any of them would even be taken alive, anyway. There was just the concern about their computers.

Nikki had a high degree of computer knowhow and was well aware that all email and instant ACU chats could be tracked by the cops. Every computer connected to the internet had an Internet Protocol Address and that worried Nikki, as these IP addresses could be traced. Even if one of his boys was killed or refused to talk, his computer would still be analyzed. The police would be smart enough to track the IP addresses of Nikki and his boys to each of their Internet Service Providers. From there it would be a cakewalk locating each of their computers and in turn each of his boys. Tracing IP addresses could ruin everything, but Nikki would not allow the cops to disrupt his boys' justice.

For this reason, before each shooting, his boys' computers must be destroyed. Nikki, being last would leave his computer intact, so he could brag beyond the grave. He would not be taken alive. Wesley, using a library computer would be the most challenging. He certainly could not destroy or steal it, but Nikki surmised that since only one day would elapse between his and Wesley's shootings the cops would not find that particular computer until after Nikki took care of his own evil boys. It was the perfect plan for taking justice.

For the next two hours, Nikki explained the plan to each of his boys. To his delight all his boys warmed up to the idea right away, like soldiers ready to fight. They were armed, they were ready, and now Nikki was letting them go. Come Monday a Week of Justice would commence.

CHAPTER 30

Sunday Night: Nikki and Gregory

*L*ogging onto *Automatic Chatting Utility*
Welcome to ACU

TheGorgeousOne: *Gregory sweetie are you there?*

M@nikM@nn: *yeah I am scared a little*

TheGorgeousOne: *I know sweetie, it's a big day tomorrow.*

M@nikM@nn: *Yeah, but I wanna do it. your proud of me right.*

TheGorgeousOne: *I am so proud of you*

TheGorgeousOne: *Your mom doesn't know anything right?*

M@nikM@nn: *No nothing, shes always in her office. I don't think she will miss me.*

TheGorgeousOne: *No sweetie she wont. She never noticed you*

TheGorgeousOne: *I will miss you but you must get justice for what you have suffered.*

M@nikM@nn: *I suffered a lot. Sooo much I want to do this. School is hell.*

TheGorgeousOne: *Life is hell*

M@nikM@nn: *yeah life is hell, but I will make there lives hell and end them.*

TheGorgeousOne: *Do you have your gun?*

M@nikM@nn: *yeah, it was in my mom's closet, she wont miss it.*

TheGorgeousOne: *I'm so proud of you and i love you very much*

M@nikM@nn: *i love you to Nikki. Can I ask you a question*

TheGorgeousOne: *You can ask me anything*

M@nikM@nn: *What will it feel like when i get justice?*

TheGorgeousOne: *It will be ecstasy the guilty will pay and you will feel a euphoria that has long been denied you. all the hurt will wash away and you will be at peace.*

M@nikM@nn: *I like that. to have peace, I never had that*

TheGorgeousOne: *I know sweetie, but you will. Now you need to get to bed and rest up. tomorrow will be the greatest day of your life. Remember though you must get rid of your computer*

M@nikM@nn: *yeah i will, i love you goodbye.*

M@nikM@nn is offline

CHAPTER 31

Justice on Monday

E ver since Gregory was a baby, he had never been a good sleeper. He'd wake up in his crib several times a night and cry for seemingly no reason. He wet the bed until he was nearly eight and, to this day, he needed a nightlight in his room. Usually, to help pass the time at night, he played videogames, but not Sunday night. He no longer needed them and they lay in a neglected pile on the floor. This night he lay awake in his bed, planning the attack. He had one Glock 17 with a single magazine holding a total of fifteen rounds. With fifteen bullets and five targets he'd have to make them all count. He had enough bullets to spare but not enough to waste and a proper plan was needed.

The lunch room was the best place to blast them. They would be sitting all together, eating their lunches. By shooting them while sitting, they would first have to get up in order to flee, but Gregory wouldn't allow that. Ray had to go first. The order of the others didn't matter and he could decide that at the last moment, but Ray, the Pack leader, absolutely had to go first. Head shots were the best shots because they were always worth the most points and it was a guaranteed kill, nobody in videogames ever survived a headshot and neither would the Pack.

Gregory smiled as he thought of the Pack, his prey. Right now they were all sleeping in their cozy little beds, unaware that it was their last night on earth. There was no hope for them. Their fates were decided and they could not be saved. There was no going back now. Nikki would be so proud of him.

Shortly before 5 a.m., after a sleepless night of planning, Gregory rose from his bed and unhooked his computer's CPU. Without it, the cops couldn't learn of any of his online chats with Nikki. She had to be protected just as she had protected him. Once unhooked from the monitor, keyboard and other components, he snuck out of the house and shuffled down the street. It was a cool morning and Gregory listened to the birds chirp their songs of the dawn, wishing him well for the day. In back of a local convenience store was a dumpster. Gregory chucked the CPU in, knowing he'd no longer need it. Monday was trash pick-up day and soon the contents of the dumpster would be crushed up in the back of a garbage truck. So much for the cops finding Nikki. He wouldn't let them.

After he arrived at school, he hid in the bushes and scanned the surroundings. There were several periods before lunch and he'd have to wait and hide from the Pack until then. Gregory needed them to be together and right now they were scattered. He spied Garrett over by the flagpole while Ray was near the bike rack. He saw someone that might have been Simon within a group of kids, but they were so clustered he couldn't be sure, and he had no clue where Eric or Caleb were. Gregory hunkered down, hoping they wouldn't be absent. All five had to be killed. That was the proper thing to do.

He waited until after the bell rang for all the other students to file into the school. Alone in the bushes, he sat amazed that a day such as today could start out so normally. Blood would be spilled today but, for the moment, all was status quo. He'd be late to his first period class but it didn't matter. All he had to do was act as normally as he could until lunch and, of course, avoid the Pack. He couldn't let the gun be found in his backpack. That would ruin everything and there was too much at stake.

His teacher, with her focus on the board, didn't no-

tice him walking into his first class tardy. It was an unex-
pected bit of luck. When she turned around and saw him,
she suspected he had just walked in, but since she hadn't
called role yet, she decided against bothering with an in-
quiry. Gregory lowered his gaze, trying to hide his smirk.
So far everything was going his way.

He could never have told anyone what was discussed
in class that period. His mind was preoccupied with other
matters. Once the bell rung, he had to be first out the door
and had to run full speed to his next class. He had to
avoid the Pack. One of their head shaking treatments
would wreck all his careful planning. Their awful improper head treatments jumbled his mind and made him
loose focus and, today, focus could not be lost. When the
bell rung, he bolted out the door and didn't look back.

So far so good, Gregory thought. He was able to
reach his bathroom ceiling locker, stepping into the bathroom right foot first, of course, and get to another period
without discovery. He had to be careful. Although he had
thus far avoided the Pack, they had spies everywhere.
Plenty of students, who knew the Pack, had seen him.
With lunch drawing near, Gregory became twitchy and
restless. He taped his fingers, licked his lips, darted his
eyes from side to side, and many other improper things
that people would notice. Sooner or later, someone would
look inside his mind and foil him. Gregory, feeling like
his own worst enemy, needed some space.

The period before lunch he decided to skip and hide in one of the stalls of his bathroom. He rocked back and forth on the toilet, reminding himself that Nikki was counting on him and ecstasy awaited. He had to remain calm for one more period then justice would be served. Missing the period was of no consequence, but the teacher would mark it down, and if they found him he'd be in trouble. Gregory rocked harder with his hands fastened together as if in prayer, hoping he would not be found before his justice.

The long-awaited bell shattered the toilet time silence and he waited an extra ten minutes in the stall, knowing it would take a little while for the Pack to gather their lunches from their lockers and arrive at the cafeteria. *That's okay*, Gregory decided. *I'm very patient and that's the proper way to be.*

Finally, he was ready. He snuck from his bathroom and trotted down the hall. It was just about time, but when he peered into the lunch room his heart nearly sank. Only three members of the Pack sat at their usual table: Ray, Eric, and Garrett. Where were Simon and Caleb? No. *No*, this wouldn't do at all. This was improper! They all had to die and they all had to be together to die. Oh God, Nikki would be fuming if he chickened out or failed to get all of them. She had given so much to him and it was time for him to give back.

His focus then shifted to the lunch line and he ex-

haled a sigh of relief. There were Simon and Caleb waiting in line for their sloppy joes. Gregory blotted the sweat
from his head, relieved he just had to wait a few more
minutes for them to sit down. They were all accounted
for. The Pack was all here.

It was just as well to delay justice for a few minutes.
Gregory's gun sat unloaded in his backpack. He entered
the bathroom nearest the cafeteria, not realizing or caring
any longer which foot entered first. Once hidden away in
a stall, he slid the magazine into the Glock, switched off
the safety, chambered a round, and pointed it toward the
stall door, testing the sights. He had the power now.

It was time to put his plan in motion. Gregory un-
tucked his shirt and gently placed the gun in his waistband, allowing the shirt to conceal it. When he got close
enough to the Pack, he would carefully lift up his shirt
with his left hand and draw the gun with his right. It was
the proper thing to do as the idea of getting the gun
caught on his shirt terrified him.

With the gun hidden, he exited the bathroom and returned to the lunch room door to sneak another peek,
hoping the other two Pack members had sat down. Gregory smiled when seeing that they had. All was proper. He
observed their seating formation and concocted the final
phase of his plan.

The Pack sat at a table with three on one side and
two on the other. With his back to the doorway of the

lunch room, Ray sat on the end with Simon in the middle and Garrett on the right. On the other side facing the door was Eric across from Ray and Caleb across from Garrett. Gregory would have to be quick. From their seating positions there was no way that Eric and Caleb wouldn't see him coming, but it didn't matter. They might see him but they'd never see what horror was coming from his pants until it was too late.

Gregory could not observe the faces of the three with their backs toward him, but he could see Eric and Caleb's. Something was funny, hilarious even. Gregory shook with rage, knowing it had to be about him. It was probably a joke made about the head shaking treatments. Well, they could enjoy their last few minutes together. Soon they'd be—

"Gregory!"

Gregory whirled around in a daze and was again face to face with the principal. He craned his head down, avoiding eye contact, and wept inside his mind, knowing that he had just blown it. He waited too long to strike and now the chance was gone forever. The principal knew that he had skipped a period and he knew about the gun. Justice was gone. He failed Nikki.

"Why are you standing out here? This is lunch time you should be in there." The principal pointed toward the lunch room.

"I—I know. I—I'm sorry," Gregory stuttered.

"If you want to stand out here a moment, okay, but then get in there, all right?"

"Okay," Gregory said.

The principal nodded and strolled on into the lunch room. He found two of the aids and began shooting the breeze with them, forgetting all about the jittery kid just outside. Gregory watched for a moment, stunned by his luck. The principal had always been reluctant to pry into his mind, but somehow he wasn't aware that Gregory had cut a class and had a gun right under his shirt. He patted the hidden gun, proud that he had shielded his mind. Justice would be his after all.

His focus returned to the Pack as he ironed out his plan one last time. He would march swiftly to the table. When close enough, he would pull his gun out and blow the back of Ray's head off. Ray had to go first, that was proper. Shock would initially befall the other four and Gregory would swivel the gun over and take out Simon with a head shot. Garrett would be next in the same manner. Once those three were neutralized, he would then aim over the table and get Caleb between the eyes and then Eric. This was the proper way of doing things. Fifteen bullets in the gun, but it should only take five shots to do the job. Bang, Bang, Bang, Bang, Bang, and justice would be served.

The moment had arrived. Gregory took a deep breath and started for the Pack. *This is for you, Nikki.* While his legs wobbled, he forced them forward and clutched his shirt, ready to draw the gun. He saw only the Pack. He heard only the Pack. All others in the lunch room faded away. Their game was about to be over.

Halfway to the table, Eric and Caleb still did not see him, too busy laughing at what whatever stupid thing Ray had said. *Good, the easiest type of prey is unaware prey.* The Pack was so used to being the hunters and now they were caught unprepared for life and death on the other side. They never watched their backs, and why should they? They never needed to before. They lacked survival skills.

Too bad for them.

At the last moment, Eric looked up, but with Ray in front of him, his view of the gun was blocked until, of course, it was drawn, placed to the back of Ray's head and fired. The blast was deafening and disorientation spread across the cafeteria as Ray's brains spread across the lunch table.

Before Simon could react, his brains too decorated the table and his corpse slumped over. Gregory, deaf to the screams, then blasted the side of Garret's head. As the third Pack member dropped to the floor, Gregory stretched the gun over the table and, as planned, planted a bullet between Caleb's eyes, flinging him backward. Gregory, momentarily distracted by the explosion out the back of Caleb's head, allowed the last pack member, Eric, to rise from the table. Screaming, waling, and covered in Ray's blood, Eric stumbled back in a disorganized escape attempt. With Eric now more than five feet away, a head shot was no longer possible. That was okay. There was now more than one proper way of doing things. Gregory stepped to his left, focused his sights on the stumbling doomed boy, and then fired round after round into him, until Eric dropped too. The Pack was dead.

Gregory stood over his justice for a moment, before reality shook him worse than Ray ever could. Screams came from everywhere as students fled the lunch room. Several students had fallen and been trampled. One student in particular caught Gregory's eye, a girl in a wheel chair had been knocked over in the stampede and lay motionless. The table and surrounding floor was coated in brains and blood. Gregory took a step, slipped, and fell into the mess.

He gasped as he pulled himself away from his handiwork, letting go of the gun. So much blood, all over. This was much more real than any videogame. Why had all the students run? he wondered. All those screams, where did they come from? He rose from the ground, still expecting Ray to bolt up and give him a head treatment, but Ray would perform those no more. With the cafeteria mostly cleared, Gregory assumed he was alone until he noticed the principal across the room, standing with his mouth agape.

"Gregory! What did you do?"

It was more a choked cough than a question, but it sent Gregory into a panic. Where the gun was now, Gregory would never know, but he charged out the emergency exit on the far side of the lunch room and just ran.

The tears burned his eyes and obstructed his vision as his feet pounded the ground like a one-man stampede. What was wrong? He had gotten his justice and surely justice should feel better than this.

Justice wasn't fear or running, it was wonderful, bliss, ecstasy. Where was the ecstasy Nikki had promised him? She never would have lied. No, not Nikki. She loved him and, yet, still he ran faster and faster, farther and farther from the school, until he ran into the path of a speeding pickup truck.

CHAPTER 32

Monday Night News

The entire nation was glued to their television sets that Monday evening and Nikki was no exception. Six boys were dead. Five had been shot, with the shooter fleeing and being struck by a truck.

Gregory took his justice and Nikki couldn't have been prouder. He loved seeing the tears of the survivors and the sobs of the rotten parents who had lost their little demons. Nikki sprawled out on his bed, wearing a little pink nighty and a wide smile.

From time to time throughout the evening, Nikki changed the channel to hear what each of the various news agencies and all the idiot talking heads had to say. All sorts of highly intelligent and well-spoken experts gave their two cents on why this had happened. Some called Gregory an evil boy, while others pointed to the dangers of bullying. Nikki found it very amusing that only a few brought up any notion of access to guns. The gun people stated that it was "too soon" and that "emotions" were still raw. Bullying was to blame. No, it was mental illness. No, no, it was violent video games. Well, it certainly had nothing at all to do with guns. That was one thing all could agree on. Oh no, six corpses lay before them, but no one could upset the gun people. Nikki rolled over and ran his hands down his freshly waxed legs.

Gregory had achieved his justice and, as long as he had gotten rid of his computer as instructed, Nikki's other two boys and he would get theirs as well. Gregory could be relied on to dump the computer as he was a good obedient boy. Like a doting mother taking pride in her son's achievement, Nikki blew a kiss to the TV whenever Gregory's odd but handsome face flashed across it.

When the names and faces of the Pack were revealed, Nikki grudgingly admitted that they were attractive boys, but still evil. Many students who had witnessed the attack cried about how wonderful they all were. They were so nice and funny and loved by everyone. Ray was a gifted baseball player, Simon was great with computers, and Garrett was shy but sweet. Oh, they were all such dolls. What a horrible thing to have happen! Few acknowledged the Packs' atrocities, and everyone eagerly denounced Gregory as a weird kid, an outsider, and a loner. Gregory was no victim to them. How dare he bring such violence and horror into their lives? How dare he disrupt their tranquility and destroy their wonderful orderly existence? How dare Gregory? He was an evil boy.

According to the principal, who neglected to mention his encounter with Gregory moments before the shooting, Gregory was an odd young man who had problems fitting in. The principal described him as decent but troubled, whatever that meant. None of the parents of the slain boys spoke to the cameras, but there was no shortage of tearful distant relatives describing their poor nephews or cousins as wonderful children, saint like even. Nikki scoffed at how little parents really knew about their children.

Nikki did wonder where Gregory's mother was, as she seemed to drop off the face of the Earth. The police mentioned speaking with her but said she was now in hiding. Perhaps Nikki could scrape up a residue of sympathy for her, but where was she while her son was stepped on? She sat in her office, focusing on her career, expecting a teen boy to fend for himself all the time. *Oh well. Now you have lots of time to work on that career of yours.*

After a few hours, Nikki grew bored of listening to the idiots on the idiot box talk and turned off the television. The news ratings would still be plenty high, even without his two gorgeous eyes watching. Ronald would need to talk very soon, but first Nikki twirled around the room in a private victory dance. He'd miss Gregory forever, but with his help this poor misunderstood boy achieved greatness, if only in Nikki's loving, maternal eyes.

"Well done, my sweet boy," Nikki whispered. "I will always love you."

CHAPTER 33

Monday Night: Nikki and Ronald

*L*ogging onto Automatic Chatting Utility…
Welcome to ACU

TheGorgeousOne: *Ronald, are you there sweetie?*

77Hercules77: *Yeah, I was watching tv for a while.*

TheGorgeousOne: *Yes, its amazing Gregory did a great job. Its your turn tomorrow sweettie*

77Hercules77: *I didnt know you talk to other boys online. Any others?*

TheGorgeousOne: *I speak to quite a few people and*

they are all special, especially you Ronald. Oh dear Ronnie Sweetie, please don't doubt that. You want justice don't you

77Hercules77: *I believe you. I kinda thought you spoke to others.*

TheGorgeousOne: *Oh of course sweettie, amazing what Gregory did today right?*

77Hercules77: *Yeah and I want my name famous like that. I want to be on the news and stuff*

TheGorgeousOne: *and tomorrow you will be, and you'll get justice for yourself. you have a gun right?*

77Hercules77: *yeah I got it from my dad's locked case. The combo was my moms birthday. there watching tv like always so they won't notice it's gone*

TheGorgeousOne: *Don't forget to get rid of your computer too*

77Hercules77: *don't worry Nikki I won't let the cops trace you through my computer. behind my house is a creek and after my parents go to sleep i'll throw it in.*

TheGorgeousOne: *good sweetie good, you have it all worked out. I am very proud of you.*

77Hercules77: *school was bad for me like always but tomorrow is gonna be great.*

TheGorgeousOne: *it will be great it will be wonderful for you. The evil boys who taunt you and make your life hell will be dealt with and you'll feel the same ecstasy Gregory did.*

77Hercules77: *yeah, Gregory must of felt great and I will too.*

TheGorgeousOne: *It will be the best moment of your life and at this time tomorrow everyone will be talking about you.*

77Hercules77: *yeah, me. They'll see me as a great soldier for justice*

TheGorgeousOne*: you better believe it Ronald. You are a soldier you've fought for so long and now finally your conquest will be complete.*

77Hercules77: *my parents will go to bed soon and I wanna get the computer unhooked and throw it into the creek I love you Nikki*

TheGorgeousOne: *I love you too, go get em Hercules*
77Hercules77: Oh *I will lol. Goodbye.*

77Hercules77 is offline

CHAPTER 34

Justice on Tuesday

Once his parents had lumbered up the stairs and plopped into their bed for the night, Ronald went to work unplugging the computer. He amazed himself at how silently he descended the stairs and opened the back door of the house. Once outside it was a very short walk to the creek, though he still had to put the computer down to rest at one point. With the little physical strength he possessed, he heaved the computer into the water and it sank to the bottom out of sight. Whether it washed downstream or just sat where it landed made no difference.

The cops would never find it and they'd never find Nikki.

With the disposal of the computer completed, another thought came to Ronald. There was something else besides the computer that needed to be lobbed into the creek, and he waddled as fast as he could up to his room to retrieve it. Tears formed in his eyes as he picked up the duffle bag filled with garbage "food," knowing it was now useless. Shame filled him as he descended the stairs for the second time. First, he was abused by others in school, then he'd come home to the duffle bag's abuse. No more. Tonight he would do away with that duffle bag forever, and tomorrow he'd do the same with Michael, Justin, and Zach. He reached the creek again and flung it in.

As the bag soared through the air to its watery grave, the zipper opened and released some of its filth into the flowing creek. The duffle bag, being lighter than the computer floated away, followed by the scattered contents. When the last bag of potato chips disappeared, Ronald wept quietly at the bank of the creek. One enemy was dead and three more would follow.

With his task completed, Ronald returned to his room and collapsed into his bed, exhausted from the night's chores. Unlike Gregory, who slept not a wink before his day of justice, Ronald passed out the moment his head hit the pillow and he slept soundly all night.

ల/ఎ౪/ఎ

He awoke at the whim of his buzzing alarm clock on Tuesday, his Tuesday. Aromas from the kitchen did little to sway him as he rolled out of bed. His parents undoubtedly were enjoying their regular breakfasts of pancakes and bacon and eggs and hash browns and biscuits with gravy and juice and coffee. Ordinarily, Ronald would have raced down in record time to gobble up some of the food while it remained, but this morning food could go to hell.

"Are you sure you don't want anything?" asked his mother.

"No, Mom, I'm not hungry, I'll just have a glass of juice."

His perplexed parents honored his wishes and gave him only a tall glass of juice, though they had made enough breakfast for him, themselves, as well as several others. He drank down the juice and then excused himself, intending to get to school early. His goal was to take care of Michael, Justin, and Zach right outside the front doors before the school day even started. He knew just where to lay in wait for them too. They'd never know what hit them.

Before leaving, Ronald fabricated a story of meeting a friend he didn't have to look over some class notes. His parents, being thrilled at the mention of the word "friend," said goodbye, pleased that Ronald was so up-beat this morning, instead of his usual sullen self.

"And he didn't even eat," remarked his mother.

His father shrugged in bewilderment and shoved another forkful of pancakes into his mouth.

"Well, he seems better today, doesn't he?" Ronald's mother asked.

"Yeah, a bit more chipper. I wish he'd had eaten at least a little something," his father replied.

Ronald's mother poured some cold OJ in her glass as she added three more pancakes to her plate. She dumped some maple syrup onto her second helping of breakfast and then some powdered sugar. She hadn't been sure there was any left after her husband had gotten a hold of it, but luckily this time he had left some.

"I just get worried about Ronald sometimes, his mother said. "He's a bit hefty and it can be tough for kids like him."

"Well, to be fair he is a growing boy," his father said.

"Oh I know," his mother continued, "but heavy children can get it hard in school."

"I'm sure Ronald is okay. He may get taunted a little, but the school would tell us if it was really bad. The fact is that he comes from a heavy family. It's just how we're built. I'm heavy, you're heavy—but none the less beauti-ful." Ronald's father cracked a smile at his joke. "Our parents were heavy, so is your sister, my sister, and their kids. "We're just big, heavy people. The problem is society. Society needs to do more to accept heavy people like us."

After the speech, Ronald's father rose from the table to use the restroom as his wife nodded in agreement and then helped herself to the last of the biscuits. She spread some gravy on it and took a big bite.

ოელი

Ronald was the first one at school and he savored the silence. Soon it would be loud, very loud. He concealed himself behind a minivan parked on the street and waited. At some point his three targets would arrive, and he'd march right up to them and leave them riddled with bullets. He could imagine their faces the moment before he pulled out his Baretta Px4Storm. They would believe it was just another day. Then a moment later, they would realize it was their last day. How happy Nikki would be. She'd be so proud of him.

Ronald carried two magazines of fourteen bullets each, more than enough for three miserable targets, and anyone else who got in his way. After loading one magazine, he placed the gun down the back of his waistband and waited. It wouldn't be too much longer. A few students were already meandering toward the school. Soon the rest would arrive for what they believed would be just another typical Tuesday.

Part of the trouble with waiting to strike was that it gave the mind a chance to reflect on all that could go wrong. The mind had a way of torturing someone into over thinking and could cause bad decisions. Ronald was aware of this on some level and did his best to combat it, but still the bad thoughts trickled in. What if they were absent? What if he dropped the gun? What if the gun jammed? What if they somehow got the gun?

Ronald pressed through the bad thoughts by focusing on his task and remembering that Nikki was counting on him. Today was his day for justice. There would be no mistakes. He kept telling himself there would be no mistakes.

One by one, the buses pulled up and delivered their students as others arrived on foot, all ready for what was to be nothing more than a normal day. Sure, there was a school shooting elsewhere the day before, but things like that could never happen here. No, today would be just another dull Tuesday.

Ronald's lungs weren't built for such exertion, and although he stood perfectly still in the safety of his hiding spot, he was struck continuously by near fainting spells. He would grow woozy, the world would spin ever so slightly, his vision would blur for a mere moment, and then it would pass. Over and over again this happened. It wouldn't be much longer. They'd arrive soon. Once they did, they would chat for a while right outside the front doors, and then he'd get them. Ronald mopped his forehead sweat with his sleeve and sucked up oxygen greedily. This was no time to pass out.

Zach arrived first and joined another group of boys in front of the school. He seemed to be his usual happy-go-stupid self as he laughed and playfully punched another boy. Ronald sneered at his happiness, but soothed himself in the knowledge that he was watching the last moments of Zach's happy life. Ronald also couldn't help but marvel at the fact that Zach seemed to have no inkling that he was living his last minutes. Ronald chuckled, easier to kill then.

The vicious Michael arrived second and joined the group at the door. He thudded what must have been a fully loaded backpack on the ground and then kicked it, another victim of his brutality. Ronald surmised the backpack deserved the kick for being too heavy. Michael hated anything that was too heavy and punished it. Everyone should be lean and athletic, just like him. He was perfection. Ronald reddened at the thought, but soon Michael would be red too, blood red.

A few more minutes later, Justin finally graced the group with his presence. At last they were together and it was time for the fun to start. Using the abundant sweat on his face, Ronald matted his hair down to ensure it would stay out of his eyes. He checked the gun for the four-teenth time before placing it back in his waistband. There was no way to sneak up on them so he'd just walk up and fire. Even if they saw him coming, they wouldn't suspect a thing. They'd think it was just another day and another game until he pulled out the heat.

Time to go.

He moved around the van and began the longest walk of his life. Upon crossing the street, he made his way up the sidewalk toward the front doors where the mass of boys stood. His gaze was steady and his body finally dry, calm. Even his hands were no longer shaking. Halfway up the sidewalk, one of the other boys in the group noticed his approach and motioned to Michael. The group all turned, still smiling, still clueless. Justin started for him first, with Zach right behind, both ready to play. Too bad it wasn't their game.

"Hey, you're not hiding today, pudgy?"

"Nope," Ronald said.

In one smooth, perfect motion, Ronald brought out the gun from behind and put a bullet through Justin's throat. Blood spattered, Justin fell, his face forever con-torted in shock. Zach turned to flee but proved unable to outrun the three bullets that pierced his back. He col-lapsed in a heap as the screams began.

It was fair to call Michael sadistic. It was fair to call him cruel, but one could never fairly call him stupid or slow. Seeing his two partners in crime fall, Michael bolted from the group of boys and, more importantly, away from Ronald. His time in power had come and gone and his life was all he had left.

Ronald swung his gun and fired. A girl was thrown back as her brains separated from her skull. Ronald fired again, hitting a teacher in the shoulder. A third bullet and another boy collapsed, grabbing his belly. Ronald fired bullet after bullet at his swift moving target and more students fell to the ground. He kept firing until the clicks revealed the gun's emptiness.

Ronald quickly slipped out the spent magazine and forced the new one in, just in time to watch the uninjured Michael vanish around the corner of the school. Ronald could never catch up. He had lost him. He stood in disbelief. He'd actually missed Michael. With Michael gone, it was only then that Ronald lowered the gun and viewed his scene.

Justin and Zach lay dead. The group of boys they had been part of had disappeared, but it was the path of Michael's escape that stole Ronald's attention. Two girls lay motionless and three other students as well as a teacher moaned on the ground. Other students huddled together too scared to move, while many had fled inside and around the building. Ronald heard screams in the distance, screams far softer than the ones in his mind.

How could he have missed Michael? How? He took

care of Justin and Zach, but how could his day of justice be complete with Michael still living? It couldn't be. He had failed. Michael was just too quick. He should have started with him. That was his mistake. Now Michael was miles away and would live forever, bragging of his survival.

Oh, how could he have screwed up so badly? Ronald wondered. How could he have let Nikki down after all she had done for him? The world began spinning as vomit exploded from his mouth. So distraught was he that he did not notice his puke landing on Justin's body. Now Nikki would hate him.

Ronald fell to his knees, sobbing, and looked at the two motionless girls lying in the grass. One hit in the head, the other in the back. He didn't even know their names. He hadn't meant to hit them. He wanted Michael. This was Michael's fault, all his fault. "I'm sorry, I'm sorry," he pleaded to the girl's bodies.

This was supposed to be his day of justice. Nikki hadn't said anything about vomiting. That couldn't be part of justice. He hadn't considered killing others besides his targets. Why hadn't Nikki warned him? She knew everything. Why didn't she warn him? Michael escaped, two girls were dead, and Nikki had lied to him! Oh God!

He heard the faint cry of sirens in the distance and another volley of barf burned its way up his throat. It was all over, everything. Nothing mattered. Ronald's last meal was the gun in his mouth and, a moment later, he joined Justin and Zach on the bloody ground.

CHAPTER 35

Tuesday Evening

The chatter of the news was music to Nikki's ears that night. Now terror began spreading across the nation. There had been two shootings in two different states in two days and the media decided that a connection was certain. Nikki delighted in the fact that Gregory and Ronald's missing computers was leaked out. Not only were Nikki and his last boy Wesley safe, the whole of America was on the verge of panic.

Nikki loved the media. They were masters of horror in ways even Stephen King could never compete with, frightening people into watching nonstop. Nikki giggled, thinking of Americans huddling close on their couches watching the news, shivering while clinging to their precious children. Report after report, hour after hour of the same thing, with various psychologists, IT experts, criminal profilers, and security management people, all playing a supporting role in a national fright fest, with Nikki as its unknown starlet.

Once Wesley took his justice tomorrow, America would really be in a panic. Several members of Congress had already issued safe and politically correct statements condemning the attacks and calling for national mourning. Prominent movie actors came forward, offering their condolences because, as Hollywood stars, their words of wisdom mattered more than the average person's.

Nikki really loved it when foreign correspondents harped over the days' events. He had meant to get the nation's attention, but never did he believe the entire world would focus solely on him. Almost giddy, he couldn't resist lying back on his bed and touching himself all over.

A half hour and a shower later, Nikki returned to the TV to see if there were any new developments. Cameras caught footage of Ronald's parents waddling into their house after a police interview. They looked as fat and stupid as Ronald described.

Nikki rolled his eyes, feeling safe. They probably didn't know what their feet looked like, much less anything about the plan. Not only that, they probably never suspected their son had any sort of problem at school. *Oh, of course not. You have a short, pudgy, weak kid among other teenagers but he'll never have any issues fitting in. Absolutely, he'll be accepted straight away. They'll even vote him prom king because kids are just so caring for each other.*

Those fat idiots had doomed their son with their disgusting habits. They looked to be the type that blamed genetics for their familial weight problems, all the while cramming as many donuts and cheese doodles into their pie holes as possible. Nikki sighed, knowing they'd find comfort at the bottom of a pit of ice cream.

From the school and community, the mood was one of standard shock, outrage, and tears. Some kid named Michael something or other was mentioned as a survivor, but a few brutally honest students revealed to the media what he was all about. Ronald had gotten two of his bullies, at least, and two other girls as well.

Gregory had done a better job in terms of precision, but collateral damage was to be expected and was acceptable. It was somewhat unfortunate but the innocent always suffered the most. Cases in point: Gregory, Ronald, Wesley, and, of course, Nikki.

Nikki was still plenty proud of his poor boy Ronald, but now there was Wesley to attend to. He checked his computer and saw that Wesley was online and ready to chat. Finally, he had gotten himself to the library.

Nikki muted the TV just as a reporter was loading on as many adjectives describing the situation as he had learned in journalism school. Hoping Wesley was as excited as he was, Nikki sat down in his pink desk chair and began typing.

CHAPTER 36

Tuesday Night: Wesley and Nikki

*L*ogging onto Automatic Chatting Utility…
Welcome to ACU

TheGorgeousOne: *Wesley are you there sweetie?*

Fi$tofCa$h: *Yeah, I was watching tv before. Now I am in the library.*

TheGorgeousOne: *amazing isn't it?*

Fi$tofCa$h: *yeah. Its my turn tomorrow right?*

TheGorgeousOne: *you bet it is.*

Fi$tofCa$h: *I kinda thought you talked to others too. That's good though, make others feel better*

TheGorgeousOne: *I care about you as much as I care about Gregory and Ronald*

Fi$tofCa$h: *I know, I just knew you would set something amazing like this up. Your so smart.*

TheGorgeousOne: *Thank you sweetie, Like I said, its all about justice.*

Fi$tofCa$h: *I know and I want it. You know what those guys did to me*

TheGorgeousOne: *They are evil boys*

Fi$tofCa$h: *yeah, but me and my shotgun will take care of business*

TheGorgeousOne: *Wonderful, I am so proud of you*

Fi$tofCa$h: *Thanks Nikki, I really want you to be happy*

TheGorgeousOne: *I am of course, two of my boys had there justice and now another will*

Fi$tofCa$h: *The cops wont find you right? I don't want that to happen.*

TheGorgeousOne: *don't worry Ronald and Gregory got rid of their computers. They can't trace it to me*

Fi$tofCa$h: *Good, but what about me. I am at a library computer, I cant just destroy it.*

TheGorgeousOne: *I've been thinking about that but I don't think I need to worry I'll be taking my own justice on Thursday. I don't think the cops will trace that computer in such a short amount of time, even if they do find it.*

Fi$tofCa$h: *I hope not, you should have justice to. Your life is hell like mine right?*

TheGorgeousOne: *yes it is. You and the other online boys were my only saving grace. I am so glad I found all of you*

Fi$tofCa$h: *I'm glad you found me too I was very sad before. I don't like my family.*

TheGorgeousOne: *Your family doesn't understand you like I do. I don't have such a great family either*

Fi$tofCa$h: *Life is unfair but it will be more fair tomorrow right?*

TheGorgeousOne: *Oh yes, those evil boys will regret ever messing with a man like you*

Fi$tofCa$h: *Thanks Nikki I love you, but I gotta go now cause the library is closing.*

TheGorgeousOne: *Ok Wesley, I love you too, go get em.*

Fi$tofCa$h: *Oh I will*

Fi$tofCa$h is offline

CHAPTER 37

Justice on Wednesday

After walking out of the library, Wesley was still uneasy about leaving the computer behind. He took some solace in the fact that the evening librarian was ancient and probably couldn't see the sun, much less him at a particular computer. At least that was what Wesley hoped. He couldn't live with himself if the police found Nikki.

God, she was brilliant, planning this scheme, allowing poor humiliated kids like him to have their days of justice. All the TV shows were talking about it, wondering if it was some kind of organized terror plot. Tomorrow they'd all see that it was indeed. Wesley grinned, honored to be able to take part in this grand event.

Knowing that the shooting would be at close range, Wesley decided on a Remington 870 Pump Action Shotgun, one of the best for home defense, as well as school invasion. His model had a six-round barrel, but Wesley would play it safe and stuff extra shells into his pockets. What he liked about his shotgun was that when fired, the buckshot pellets spread out, making it easier and more likely to hit your target. To keep himself organized, he wrote a short hit list: Scotty, Kyle, Taylor, Barry.

A buckshot blast from a shotgun was usually enough to make a kill with one round. It certainly would, if the target was struck in the head or torso, and even if a limb was hit, chances were they'd bleed to death, anyway. Wesley nodded to himself, satisfied with his choice of weapon.

After finally arriving home from the library, he entered the trailer to see his father passed out on the sofa, while his mother slept in her bed, a used ashtray on a small table to her right. His brothers and sisters were also asleep on the floor as the drone of the television sang lullabies. After locating the shotgun lying in the corner of the room near one of his sleeping brothers, Wesley loaded it with the shells and packed it in a seafood-stinking duffle bag he had fished from a dumpster. Now, he would give them a real stink to talk about.

After giving his mess of a family one last glance and feeling nothing, he and his duffle bag wandered outside to the hammock. It creaked and rocked under his weight, but it held, and neither the few tears nor ragged smell did anything to diminish the calm enveloping him. It was a decent night to spend under the stars, to lie there with only two thoughts in mind: the justice that tomorrow would bring and Nikki. No thoughts of his precious magazines entered his head. They were just ratty wads of paper shoved underneath his garbage heap of a bed. Maybe one of his siblings would enjoy them, but to Wesley they were now just trash.

ഇൽ

He rose early that Wednesday morning, intent on getting to school and waiting at his locker for them. Taking care of business early was a must, seeing how walking around school all day with a shotgun was risky. He would wait at his locker, they'd come along, probably say something about the stinky duffle bag, then he would whip out the shotgun, and four blasts later it would be done, simple and sweet.

The unfortunate reality of simple plans was that they rarely were so simple. In many cases, unforeseen logistical issues arose or other unanticipated events, which caused a simple plan to become skewed. Wesley had no idea just how skewed his simple plan would become.

That morning, he stood at his open locker, his eyes darting around the hall, looking for his targets. The duffle bag stank his feet, as many students walked by sporting cringed faces and flared nostrils. Plenty of remarks about the smell hit his ears, but his targets were nowhere to be seen. This would be only the first example of how a simple plan could go awry. He waited past the ringing of the bell, but they still hadn't shown up.

Wesley, infuriated by his luck and on his last nerves, started for his first period class. Although alone in the hall now with only the long rows of lockers as company, he was sure that any minute his shotgun would be discovered and he would be hauled off to jail. He'd look like a fool and fail Nikki. Every day they made his life hell, and the one day he had a surprise waiting for them, they were nowhere to be found. How could all four of them be absent on the same day? It was as if someone had tipped them off.

That last thought stopped Wesley in his tracks. Had they been tipped off? Impossible. He hadn't told anybody and, besides, if they had been tipped off, chances were they would have reported it to the police, and he would have been arrested already. It wasn't as if a tip of a planned school shooting would have been ignored. Not with Gregory and Ronald's shootings so fresh in everyone's minds. No, the police would have come out in full force to stop Wesley had they known anything about it. Wherever they were, it had to be coincidence. They couldn't know.

The teacher barely noticed when Wesley walked in late and took his seat. Several students around him eyed the duffle bag, but Wesley assured himself that it was just to identify the source of the smell, nothing more. There were four empty seats in the middle of the room, telling Wesley he was totally screwed. He bit his lip, fearing they must have cut school, today of all days. It wasn't fair, he was ready today and they wrecked his plans. Now he had to lug a shotgun around school without arousing suspicions all day and bring it back tomorrow. He slumped in his seat, hoping Nikki would understand.

For the next ten minutes or so, Wesley zoned in and out as the teacher rambled. After this class, Wesley would try to stuff the bag and shotgun into his locker, as it really did stink, and then leave it there until tomorrow. Nikki would understand. He couldn't kill who wasn't there and, besides, they'd probably be back tomorrow. And then he'd get justice for sure. A moment after he decided to postpone his plan for a day, his four targets entered the classroom, accompanied by the old crone who had chewed him out after he had pushed Kyle into the lockers.

"I'm very sorry they're late. These four nice boys were helping me move some boxes," the crone said.

"Quite all right," said the teacher and the four sat down.

Before leaving the room, the crone waved and thanked them again for the helpful muscle they provided. Her gaze caught Wesley and the smile vanished, a fact not lost on the four of them. She rolled her eyes and exited leaving the "nice boys" cackling in silence.

Having received this pleasant surprise, Wesley's plan was back on. The teacher went back to the board as Wesley stared at his duffle bag on the floor. How should he do this? Should he pull it out and just start firing? Should he wait until after class? He had planned to get them in the hallway but then again, the shotgun might be discovered if he waited too long.

As Wesley pondered his predicament, Scotty began producing spitballs and Taylor began the drawing of the day. Kyle rummaged through his bag looking for a rubber band to flick while Barry watched to make sure the teacher noticed nothing. Wesley's attention darted back and forth between his desk and the duffle bag, considering when would be the proper timing, the classroom or in the hall. The adrenaline surge started when they unexpectedly walked in and couldn't be shut down, but was this the best place for a massacre?

All of the sudden, a wet wad slapped him in the face, right below his eye. It was none other than Scotty's spitballs. Wesley had been so wrapped up in planning the deaths of his targets, he had forgotten that they were still alive. *To hell with planning. Just do it*!

He reached down and snatched the duffle bag. Wesley then rose from his seat and walked around three rows of students toward Scotty and the others as the apprehension in the room rose.

Even the teacher noticed this sudden movement. "Wesley, what are you doing?"

Wesley ignored the irrelevant teacher and his stupid question. Except for Scotty, blinders blacked out the world. Once next to him, Wesley allowed the duffle bag to drop to the floor with a thud.

"What are you doing, Wesley?" Scotty asked, looking at the other three targets as if they had answers. Wesley ignored the question and unzipped the bag. He pulled out the gun, pumped it ready, placed the barrel an inch from Scotty's face, and pulled the trigger.

The blast reverberated throughout the room as Scotty's head exploded like a cantaloupe struck by a sledge hammer. Wesley, temporarily blinded by the blood detonation, stumbled back. He quickly rubbed blood from his eyes and spat brains from his mouth. He hadn't seen that coming and, as his vision returned to normal, he began hearing the screams.

Taylor, Kyle, and Barry dashed for the door like panicked rabbits, but Wesley began blasting away, one shell after another. Several students, including Taylor, collapsed into a pile. Some in the pile were hit, while others had just fallen with them. A few students jumped out the open window as others huddled on the floor. Wesley rushed toward the door, though Taylor was down, Kyle, Barry, and several others managed to scoot out.

Taylor wailed as he clutched his nearly severed leg. Several buck shots had struck his left knee and now it dangled from the rest of his body. Wesley stumbled over and fired one more round but, being off balance, most of the round hit Taylor's right arm rather than his chest or head. Wesley began reloading and charged out the door as Taylor gaped at his nearly amputated right arm, his drawing arm.

Wesley had been around guns his whole life, making reloading as easy as slipping on a pair of pants. Several students, including Kyle and Barry, ran for their lives down the hall. Wesley fired twice, dropping three students, one of them Kyle. Barry kept running and turned the corner as Wesley approached.

One student's brains were splattered across the hall, while the other held his rear end in agony. Kyle was shot in the hip and pleaded pointlessly for his life, "Please, Wesley, Please, I'm sorry—"

One last merciless shot to the head ended the pleas. Wesley observed the other wounded student but paid him no more attention. Barry was still on the loose.

At that moment, a young student teacher, having

heard the commotion in the hallway, opened her class-room door. She never found out what was going on. Her sudden appearance on the scene startled Wesley and he fired a quick point blank round into her chest, sending her flying backward into the room. Wesley roared in frustration and took off after Barry.

He would not escape! That would not happen! Wesley had gotten three of them already and Barry would make four. Dealing with Kyle had given Barry a bit of time to gain distance and now Wesley had lost sight of him. He flew by other students in the hall, all jumping out of the way at the sight of the bloody shotgun-wielding madman. Where was Barry? He couldn't just vanish.

Wesley ran from hallway to hallway, seeking Barry, but never saw him again. Barry had, in fact, vanished. Wesley ducked into a bathroom to catch his breath and, only then, did he view himself in the mirror. What did he just do? Oh yes, he got three of them, but missed the fourth. He also had killed several others as well. He hadn't meant to. Oh my, how did that happen? he asked himself.

He stood in the bathroom, drenched in blood not his own, and stared at his living corpse in the mirror. He was dead. Nikki didn't mention this was his day to die, too. This was his day, wasn't it? It was his day for justice, but his own life was ending as well. He turned from the mirror and let off some tears. Nothing went as planned. It was supposed to be a simple four-shot volley, and that was it. How could he have forgotten? How could he have forgotten that when the buckshot spread, it increased the chance of hitting a target as well as non-target? He should have used a rifle. Oh God, he should have used a rifle.

He had to get out of there, the bathroom, the school, he had to be alone and sort out his thoughts. The field with the apple trees, yes, that's where he'd go. He exited the bathroom and jogged down the hall toward the door, just realizing the fire alarm had been pulled. Around the next corner was the exit. He could just slip out of the school, run toward the field, and hide for a while. That was a good plan. It was simple, he could do it.

He had neared the exit when a burly cop emerged from around the corner. Their surprise was mutual and both instinctively drew their guns on the other. Wesley was the faster draw, however, and blew the cop's throat out. His corpse was flung against a row of lockers as a second cop entered Wesley's view. The second cop had his gun drawn and he put bullet after bullet into Wesley.

CHAPTER 38

Wednesday Night

Wednesday evening was grand. Without any confirmation from the police, the media concluded that the three shootings were connected and, if the media says something, it is automatically true. Even the President of the United States broke his silence on the issue, saying it was "highly probable these three teen boys were organized."

Nikki smirked. *You better believe it, Mr. Prez.*

Wesley had killed nine people, including a cop, and injured fifteen others. Not all were the evil boys who terrorized Wesley. Nikki knew that, but still, whoever stood silent and allowed evil to continue deserved whatever fate befell them.

Good boy, Wesley. You have had your justice.

Unofficial, but nevertheless, highly important news polls showed that a good chunk of America was planning to keep their precious babies home from school for the next few days, although police were "working round the clock" on this case, and various federal agencies, such as the FBI and ATF were actively involved.

Nikki twirled around the room, marveling at his brilliance. One lonely teen boy from Bumblescum, Ohio, had brought about a wave of terror throughout the nation. Such a strong nation and, yet, when their babies were in danger, they became as helpless as newborns.

Nikki turned to the large American flag affixed to his wall and gave a mock salute. "God Bless America," he said and stuck out his tongue. He giggled, only half meaning his disrespect. America was a great nation without a doubt. Just like anywhere else in the world, though, America would screw you over. But there was one important difference between America and other nations that Nikki delighted in. Guns. In other countries, guns could be hard to come by, hence justice difficult to get. In America, however, if someone was ever wronged, all one need do was pick up and gun and make it right. God Bless America!

Nikki stood naked in front of the mirror holding his

pink handled Taurus .22 Pistol. He had stolen it from his great aunt during a visit several months back. The woman was so scatterbrained and disorganized, she never noticed it was missing. Now it and the two eight-round magazines were going to help Nikki take his own justice. After which, the police would come to his room, find his computer, and learn all about his brilliance. In death, he would gloat before the world as the police, the government, and the nation scratched their heads and asked how. How could one teenage boy create so much terror? It was simply too delicious.

He missed his boys, but the fact that he had helped them achieve justice, and the reality that Thursday was his turn, helped quiet the mourning inside him. Now it was his last night on this trash hole of the planet, and in less than twenty-four hours, he too would be at peace with his boys. They were all too good for the world. And what was the world if not an insignificant speck of hate hurtling through space at a bazillion miles per hour?

Tomorrow would be a great day not only to celebrate his boys' victories but his own as well. At the moment, however, it was time for a night of joy. Nikki bobbed and styled his hair, donned his makeup to perfection, brushed his pearly whites, and slipped into his favorite outfit, the prom dress. If only he could be buried in it, but alas, his parents would never allow it. What a wonderful look, what a beautiful feel. If not for the horrifying notion of it being bloodied, Nikki would happily wear it during his justice.

He pranced and posed for the mirror, marveling at his beauty and ignoring his bruises. *All boys should be so lucky*. He gave himself a flirty smile and shook his rear. He twirled for the mirror once more and watched the hem of the dress flutter around him. What happiness and peace—just him, a dress, and a mirror. What more was needed?

Nikki skipped to his dresser and retrieved the gun. Somehow it made him sexier, like a goddess no less. He held it close to his face as if he was one of Charlie's Angels. He then held it over his heart while gazing at the American flag. At that moment, a hard rapping on his door stole his attention away from the gun, the dress, and the flag. All he had time to do was hide the gun behind his back and await the inevitable.

As expected, the door opened without the intruders on the other side being given permission to enter.

"Nikki, we need to have a talk," his father started as the door grew wider.

Nikki froze in front of the mirror, wondering how his parents would react. When his eyes met those of his father, wide-eyed revulsion was all Nikki received. His mother saw the gorgeous boy in all his glory a moment later and joined in the open mouthed horror. They knew he was feminine, but they never had seen him in a dress.

"What the hell, Nikki!" his father yelled. "What the hell is this?"

His father slammed his fist against the door, flinging it into the wall, and stepped farther into the room. Nikki backed into a corner as the evil man approached, while still clutching the gun behind his back.

"This is my fault," his father said. "I was too lax, but I'll straighten you out now!"

With nowhere to go and his mother frozen in the doorway, Nikki tightened his grip on the pistol. When his father was within a few feet, Nikki whirled the gun around and put a bullet through his father's forehead. The failed paternal figure was flung backward to the floor as the squeaky maternal figure screamed.

It was more of a shriek than a scream, one that could drown out the collective laments of the mothers who would mourn their sons the following day. Nikki sprang from his corner and nearly tripped when stepping on his slain father's crotch.

Once in position, he unloaded four shots into his mother's chest. She stumbled backward from the doorway into the hall and, finally, down the stairs, crashing into a small table at the bottom.

The screaming ended. The yelling ended. The limitless hostility and mock tolerance ended. Nikki looked down at his father and saw only a wide eyed corpse. From the top of the stairs, he saw the balled up body of his mother lying in a pool of blood. Nikki returned to his room and gently placed the gun on his night table.

Upon stepping before the mirror again, he realized how heavily he was breathing and how badly mussed his hair had gotten. His hands shook, and his forehead sweated. He was a mess, but when he gave a closer look, he realized how lucky he was. Not one drop of blood had gotten on his dress.

CHAPTER 39

Justice on Thursday?

Nikki slouched on a bench in the hall, waiting for the evil boys to find him. The fresh magazine was loaded and the gun awaited its tasty prey. Sitting on a different bench were his crushes, Joel and Ashleigh, as beautiful as ever. Joel wore simple blue jeans and a T-shirt, which Nikki thought could have been tighter.

Ashleigh wore a to-die-for yellow sun dress, the hem of which hypnotized Nikki each time she twirled. It was nice seeing them one more time before the evil boys came along. The giggly couple laughed with their friends, unaware that Nikki existed. It didn't matter, anyway. Soon they'd be fleeing the bullets.

The first and, most important, thing Nikki did after slaying his parents was remove his dress and return it to the closet. He almost shed a few tears, seeing how he'd never wear it again, but now he no longer needed it. His impending justice was all that mattered. Nikki dragged his mother into the living room and laid her on the sofa. There was no need to leave her in a puddle of blood. She deserved a little better than that. Moving his overweight father was a far more daunting task. At first, Nikki was inclined to just leave him on the floor, but not wanting to sleep in the same room as a corpse, it was necessary to move him. It proved too burdensome to pull his father all the way into in the master bedroom. Instead, Nikki settled for dragging him into the bathroom and just allowing him to rot next to the toilet. Problem solved. After moving the bodies, Nikki was bushed and took a hot shower, followed by bed.

He slept well and now his Thursday had finally arrived. He'd given his boys their justice first, but now it was his turn. With that thought, his mascara-lined eyes caught sight of the evil boys approaching. They were together again after briefly being short Ethan, but having recovered, he was back and ready for action.

"Well, faggot, you gave me a concussion and I'm gonna make it my mission to beat your ass every day."

Ethan had been saying that a lot lately and those words have been backed up by endless abuse. He missed only a few days of school and, while he was gone, the evil boys had backed off a bit, but with his return, the days had been worse than ever and Nikki had the bruises to prove it. At that point, Albert stepped forward in front of Ethan, ready to state his piece. Nikki looked up from his bench but only listened out of morbid curiosity. There was nothing for him to say to Albert or the other two, but the gun was mighty anxious to get a word in.

"You know what I'm gonna do to you today, faggot?"

"Before you tell me, Albert," Nikki started, as he lowered himself to the floor and unzipped his backpack. "I have something to show you in here."

"What?" Albert asked. "Your tampon?"

The three evil boys laughed and Nikki joined in.

"No, silly," Nikki said, and he reached in.

Keeping his eyes locked with Albert's, he pulled the gun from his backpack, placed the barrel to Albert's crotch, and fired.

Albert dropped to the floor, wailing, as Nikki turned the gun on Nate and put a bullet in each knee. With equal speed, he rose to his feet, over the howling evil boys, and put three more rounds into Ethan's chest. Nikki then stepped back for a moment and admired his handiwork, oblivious to the stampeding students around him. As he was already dead, Ethan was the lucky one. Now it was playtime for the other two.

Albert groaned as he clutched his obliterated manhood and Nate began crawling for his life. Nate would be dealt with in a moment. He was getting nowhere fast with his mangled knees. Albert needed his attention first.

"Aww, poor baby," cooed Nikki. "Does that hurt?"

"Nikki—I'm sorry—I'm sorry," Albert cried.

"Aww, that's okay, Albert. I forgive you." Along with his forgiveness, Nikki gave Albert another bullet, this time into his hands, which were holding his gushing, red crotch.

Albert screamed again as Nikki grinned. "Oh God, Nikki. Please. I never—I never..."

"Never what?" Nikki asked sweetly. "Killed me? Well, too bad you didn't."

A final bullet to Albert's head ended his sobs, at which point, Nikki discarded the old magazine and replaced it with the partially used one. There were three bullets left and Nikki would put them to good use as there was still Nate to finish off.

The last evil boy, using only his arms, managed to drag himself more than fifteen feet from the other two. His knees were destroyed but his arms worked double time in his futile attempt at salvaging his life. The hall was empty, minus two and a half corpses, soon to be three. Nikki couldn't help but be amused by Nate, who was slinking along, kind of like a mortally wounded snake. He watched quietly from behind for a moment before cutting in front and stopping Nate in his slithering tracks. Their eyes met and Nikki gave him a warm beautiful smile, said, "Hi, sweetie," and then shot him in the head.

With Nate's demise, Nikki was truly alone. Distant screams were just barely audible but he wasn't concerned with that. He was content to stand quietly for a moment and wait for the feelings of justice to hit him. Any moment now, the euphoria would set in. He was sure of it. Nikki looked down at Nate and watched ooze spew from his skull. Ethan was also motionless over by Albert who had paid a really high price. Nikki viewed the evil boys for several more moments, becoming increasing perplexed. Where was the justice? Where was that feeling he promised for his boys as well as to himself? He should have felt it by now. Dammit, he had earned it. Why couldn't he feel it?

Looking at his three victims now caused protests from his stomach and Nikki turned away. Something was wrong. There had to be. His body should be rippling with happiness. All his hate should have been melting away under the warm rays of justice. Something must have gone wrong. Perhaps one of them was still alive. Yes, that was it. He subconsciously knew that one had managed to survive the shooting and, hence, justice had not been completed yet. Of course, that had to be it.

Nikki quickly checked over Nate. No, he was dead, all right. Albert was next and more brains had leaked from his head than could possibly still be inside. Perhaps Ethan was still alive. Yes, it had to be Ethan! No…Ethan was dead, too. The bullets had seared through his lungs and heart. The evil boys were dead, yet justice was denied.

The hall began spinning and Nikki stumbled away, needing to put distance between him and their bodies. Even in death, they tormented him and he was denied what was rightfully his. Nikki found his way around a corner and lost view of the bodies. To his right was a janitor's closet with the door slightly ajar. Wanting to get out of the hall, he stepped inside and closed the door. He moaned and tried to clear the fog that was fast enveloping him.

A low gasp from behind sent his arm flinging out and firing a bullet. There was a boy and a girl who had taken shelter in the closet when the shooting started, now they shared it with Nikki. It was Joel and Ashleigh and they huddled together on the floor in tear soaked terror. The bullet had flown over their heads missing them, but the fright sent Ashleigh deeper into Joel's embrace, as if she was burrowing into his chest.

Remembering that there was only a single bullet remaining in the gun, Nikki lowered it and viewed the pair at his feet. Fate had given him what he always wanted, the two of them where they were now, but there was no pleasure for anyone from their captivity, only fear. Nikki had never wanted them to be afraid.

"Nikki, we—we never hurt you," Joel said.

His glassy blue eyes captured Nikki's and drew him to the back of the closet. He turned the gun away from the pair of terrified beauties and reached toward them with his free hand. Ashleigh held her breath as Nikki lovingly stroked her hair. For how long had Nikki wanted to touch her?

Joel was next and he looked down obediently when Nikki caressed his mane. Even cringing on the floor of a janitor's closet, they were beautiful. In another world, in another life, they could have been so happy together.

Nikki backed away from them and flung the closet door open. "Get out!" he bellowed.

The couple hesitated for a moment but then fled to freedom when Nikki barked the order again. Joel practically carried Ashleigh out and clearly thanked Nikki with his eyes as they passed. With the couple out of his closet, Nikki again slammed the door closed and slid down on the floor.

All was clear. Justice didn't exist, not for him and not for his boys. How badly he had led them, all the while thinking he was caring for them. They were dead now and so was he. Nikki had known that his life was ending with these shootings but he hadn't cared until now. The denial of justice forced him to care, and that overwhelmed him.

At that moment, his eyes began to burn and his vision blurred. The long absent tears forced their way through all the barriers that had held them back for so long. Nikki had assumed that they had dried up forever, but now they ran down his face and filled his mouth. Their saltiness enflamed his cheeks and stung his unexpecting tongue. Nikki wailed and the flood came. So intense a wave, he shuddered throughout his body and keeled over on his side. On the concrete floor of a janitor's closet, he mourned. He mourned his parents. He mourned his boys. He mourned his life, his future. This wasn't him. He could have been nice. He could have had friends. He could have laughed, but no, this was all he had now.

Nikki had not gotten justice, but mourning. He had a gun, too, with one bullet. It wouldn't be long before the police would find him.

He couldn't go to jail. The evil men in there would be worse than the evil boys, and his beauty would be destroyed. No, Nikki would not go to jail. He sat up once again and placed the gun to his head.

He was about to pull the trigger when something stopped him. How would it look with his beautiful face splattered all over? That's what a bullet to the head would do. Instead, he lowered the gun and pointed the barrel over his heart. This was a better option. Nikki then pulled the trigger and relieved the pain forever.

EPILOGUE

Michael

Why she did it was anyone's guess, but during Ronald's rampage, Lady Luck had decided to pay Michael a visit. Bullets whizzed by him and struck others, but he was not so much as grazed. After escaping Ronald's wrath, Michael bounded into a local grocery store and hid out in the bathroom, where the police later found him.

Initially, he was hailed as a lucky survivor of a rampage but, within days of the shooting, other students began speaking out—not condoning Ronald, by any means, but acknowledging that Michael was no victim and was not worthy of pity. In less than a week, Michael went from finding comfort wherever he went to being jeered.

His accomplices, Justin and Zach, lay dead, as did Ronald. Michael soon found himself the piñata on which everyone vented their rage. Questions were asked, such as what kind of students would stand by as Ronald was being tormented and what kind of administration would allow it. The students, faculty, and even Ronald's parents needed to point the finger somewhere and Michael was a tangible target. A flurry of lawsuits followed. Some were directed at the school, some at Ronald's parents, and others toward Michael. The courts became increasingly overloaded with work, as Michael found himself increasingly on the outs at school. Once popular, now a popular target of blame.

The school reopened several weeks later and many of the students returned once again. Students who hardly knew one another would now embrace and circles of friends grew larger. Michael found himself forever left outside the ever widening circle, continuously pushed back as it expanded. The boys no longer high-fived or laughed with him. The girls no longer giggled or leaned in close. Michael was alone in a crowded school of mourning.

One day, a Tuesday, he just stopped showing up, preferring to stay in the basement of his father's house and strum his guitar or sit at the computer, trying to find some comfort from chat rooms. He stopped playing sports. He stopped hanging with friends. He just stopped. He started eating, playing videogames, and rarely ventured outside. He had a mirror to look into. He saw his junk-food-filled belly, his chubby face, his sun-deprived, pasty skin, and it all was appallingly familiar.

ოოო

Barry

Barry's survival was due to the fact that what he lacked intellectually, he made up for in running fast. As Kyle was being executed, Barry had found an exit from the school and ran all the way home. He told his parents everything, sparing no details about the shooting or the bullying that preceded it.

Barry's parents saw the writing on the wall and knew that, like Barry had done, it was time to flee. As soon as they were able, they packed their things, changed their last name, left South Carolina, and fled west, not stopping until they hit California. In doing this, the family dodged much of the flack that flew in. In California, most people were not aware of who they were and Barry's family was very protective of that secret.

Barry continued attending high school and joined the track team, earning a scholarship to college. His parents were eternally grateful, seeing how they had spent most of their money, including their retirement funds and 401Ks, fleeing South Carolina. Barry simply allowed his old life to drift away and slowly it receded into the deep recesses of his mind.

In college, he was a track star and the big man at many campus parties. He lived Scotty's college dream of majoring in booze and minoring in pussy, on occasion doubling up in the minor. With his arsenal of solid Cs behind him, he continued to dominate college track and, upon graduation, he had a job at his father's new business waiting for him.

ⱏⱏⱏ

Taylor

Taylor survived the shooting at the cost of an arm and a leg. He knew as he was being rushed to the hospital afterward that he had lost his left leg. As his mind swirled in its semi-conscious state, he had just enough sense to wonder whether or not he would also lose his right arm. After awaking from emergency surgery, the first thing he saw was his left arm, and the first thing he didn't see was his right. He was alive, but minus his most precious limb.

Immediately, the hate seeped in. He hated Wesley. He hated Scotty and Kyle, and he really hated Barry, alive and intact. Taylor never returned to school, nor did he ever see Barry again. His life became about bed. He lay in bed, he ate in bed, he pissed in bed. His two stumps slowly healed as his rage consumed him more and more. He refused to use a wheelchair, refused therapy, and refused any comfort that his family and friends tried to bestow. He built up iron-studded brick walls around himself, and nobody was going to break through.

For months, Taylor refused to accept any accountability for what had happened. He didn't do very much. It was the other three, especially Barry. When confronted about the drawings, or taunting with food, or marking up Wesley's face, Taylor became angry and cursed the person who'd mentioned it. At times, he became violent and, with his one good arm, threw things, once narrowly missing his own mother with a lamp.

Nothing, and nobody, could get through to Taylor until a few days before Christmas when pneumonia got through and settled in his lungs. He was rushed to the hospital, started on antibiotics, and given a fifty-fifty chance. For the next few days, he was watched over by his family. Even Barry sent a card. For months, Taylor had wanted to die, but on Christmas Day fate decided that he would live. The pneumonia was beaten back and, for the second time in a year, he had beaten the odds.

Taylor exited the hospital New Year's Day and decided he was going to try. He was going to try to live. He entered therapy and began strengthening what remained of his body. Within weeks, he could operate a motorized wheelchair, feed himself without assistance, use the bathroom, and bathe himself. By summer, he began the process of learning to use prosthetic limbs and, that fall, he got his GED, entered community college, and began learning to draw again, using his left arm. He began his own online art gallery which caught the attention of several museums. In addition, he also began an anti-bullying crusade, using himself as a model. These days, Taylor keeps busy with his art and his lectures. He speaks to everyone from students, to artists, to school officials, to members of Congress.

Taylor recently got married and exchanged vows with his bride while standing at the altar on a prosthetic leg. In the breast pocket of his tux he held a picture of Wesley and always keeps it near. Every year on the anniversary of the shooting, Taylor visits Wesley's grave and leaves him an unopened bag of Doritos.

About the Author

A moderately proud native of New Jersey, Daniel Shebses is a fresh voice in the world of bully violence. His first novel, *The Online Boys*, paints a disturbingly plausible cyber-satire, spanning the lives of three teenage outcasts and a mysterious Internet predator posing as their friend and confidant.

Beside writing, Shebses enjoys reading, CrossFit, and eating cheesecake—very often in that order. After living in Wyoming for three years, he now currently resides in the mid-western corn state of Iowa.